ʟ Night Doctor of Richmond

ALSO BY TONY GENTRY

The Coal Tower - novel

Last Rites - stories

Yearnful Raves - poems

WWII Mortarman - history

Young Adult Biographies

Paul Laurence Dunbar

Jesse Owens

Dizzy Gillespie

Alice Walker

Elvis Presley

THE NIGHT DOCTOR OF RICHMOND

A BIOGRAPHICAL NOVEL

TONY GENTRY

NExTExT
books

For the outsiders

What is this world?
What but a spacious burial-field unwall'd,
Strew'd with death's spoils,
The spoils of animals savage and tame,
And full of dead men's bones!
—Robert Blair, *The Grave*

Who is among you that feareth the Lord,
that obeyeth the voice of His servant,
that walketh in darkness, and hath no light?
—*Isaiah*, 1, 10

Monsters are real; ghosts are real, too.
They live inside us and sometimes they win.
—Stephen King

THE NIGHT DOCTOR OF RICHMOND

Medical College of Virginia, Richmond, 1867
(later known as the Egyptian Building)

PROLOGUE

We arranged to meet, the reporter said, in his quarters at the medical school, in the basement of the old Egyptian building, and I must say in all my years in Richmond those are not portals I had ever wished to darken! Butter in my rum, will you barman? Have you passed by there of late, the entire edifice clothed in ivy, up its columns, along its walls, as if mother nature herself seeks to pull the crumbling monstrosity down to the grave? Yet this structure, they say, is the chief medical college of the South, so in I went in search of my interview.

The tiled floors with their hieroglyphic inlays gleamed, the new electric lights of the wall sconces shone without a flicker, but already in the portico my nose piqued at the odor, oh my – part pig-stye, part pharmacy, part abattoir – all stirred in together. I had been warned, pulled out a quite heavily perfumed handkerchief, and held it to my face as I turned down the stairwell. Now, you who walked the bloody crater at Petersburg know well the charnel house of war, but we youngsters, I must admit that fetid stench was too much for me.

I stopped halfway to the basement and called out for him. From the murk below his face appeared, lantern-lit, gleaming and dark, except for a snatch of white beard. Those confounding eyes people

1

have spoken of, piercing and blank, peered up at me. He came up the steps to greet me in his butcher's apron and skull cap, led me further upstairs to the anatomy theater with its impressive skylight, on this bright morning not at all the horror I had supposed, more like a court-room with a half circle of benches around examination tables, all in order, no one else about. He gestured for me to take a seat, pulled up a rocker and lit a pipe, which did in some way help mitigate the aura of decay that seemed to hang in a fog about the place.

He coughed frequently. Imagine the life he has lived inside those unwholesome walls! But his answers were frank, his gaze even and direct, his manner calm, a man at peace it seemed in his occupation. Isn't that odd, knowing as we do, what he is?

Oh yes, no qualms a'tall, admitted quite candidly to snatching, he guessed, hundreds of bodies from the cemeteries hereabouts over his long career. Said he has done what was needed, takes some pride in his knowledge of anatomy, which Doctor Tompkins has told me exceeds that of his own demonstrator. I asked if it bothers him that he is shunned, treated as a sort of ghoul, in his community. At that he gave no reply, simply pulled at his beard, a slight smile, I thought, playing at his lips. We spoke for an hour before he demurred, saying there was work to be done downstairs. He invited me down, but it was then my turn to demur! Yes, I have the piece in draft, one thousand words, of course, by deadline tonight.

I must say, I don't know that I have ever met a character such as this Chris Baker. Upon taking his leave, freed again to the bracing air of Marshall Street, I found myself stumbling as if in a trance alongside the trolley tracks, clear out past the penitentiary to Hollywood Ceme-tery. There I stood amidst the many thousand tombs of our Confed-erate dead, gazing back at our fair city from a hilltop overlooking the James, and realized that my body entire was shaking, had been quiv-ering like a tuning fork, that whole somnambulistic stroll. The strangest thing, wouldn't you say? As I speak to you now, this toddy trembles in my hand.

Chapter 1

Richmond, Virginia - 1857

His mother had gone out while he was sleeping, but he found a fatback biscuit she'd left for him under an overturned frying pan on the stove. He guessed that his father was upstairs, mopping the dissection lab or salting the front steps. He ate the biscuit absent-mindedly while wandering about the basement workshop, where a human torso, ribs splayed apart, lay dripping on a butcher block, a product of the previous day's anatomy exam. The poor man's head stared up from a bucket, eye holes empty, a braid of hair from his last living day hanging over the lip. Cats lapped at the sticky floor.

The boy pulled on his boots and wool seaman's coat, a hand-me-down from a medical student that his mother had cut down to size, more or less, and went out the back door, not looking for her, just bored and seeking fresh air. Christmas Eve, unseasonably warm, the city oddly quiet, too, all the usual clanging background noise of the foundries and factories by the river stilled for the holiday. But along the steep hill down to Shockoe Creek, all went on as usual. Last week's icy rain had flooded the pauper's field, upturning shallow graves.

He crouched in the shadow of a pig stye on the slope and

gazed across the swampy gorge, watching the animals feed. A motley pack of dogs fiercely defended their meal from a pair of pushy hogs, taking turns he noticed in facing off against their opponents, then tore off chunks of flesh that they choked down as if this were their last meal. Other hogs, unmolested, tugged out whole corpses by their legs and wasted no time in rooting at the rotten innards. Already the buzzards were up from their roosts, living shadows circling, scoping out their prospects from the air. When the dogs were done, the birds teetered down one by one, formed a posse not so different from the students gathered around a cadaver in the dissection theater, he thought, and proceeded to delicately pick at leftovers in the muck. Teams of rats scurried to and fro. Thrilling when a red-tailed hawk swooped down and hauled one off screaming in its talons.

It was early yet. The children he thought of as his friends had not come to do their daily scavenging for scraps here at the dumping ground. The slaves to market had not emerged yet from their stalls, chained together at the neck, for their trodding exercise walk around the paddock. He thought he'd wander that way, enjoying as he did the sullen songs they moaned as they marched. He unbuttoned his coat and picked along in the mud, enjoying his relative freedom, and at ease in the routines of his neighborhood. Maybe he would find a shiny buckle or lapel pin upturned here, a Christmas gift for his mother.

She would soon be home with their holiday meal, a rare feast of chicken, and he would help her pluck it. Tomorrow, stacked on his stool by the cook stove, he would find gifts from the students – a broken watch, a torn hat, darned socks, and left-over cake from their end of semester celebration – and his father would pull from his vest the carving he had been whittling all month, some mythical beast to go with the others in the boy's holiday collection, the one with huge flapping ears and a nose like a hose, another with a neck as long as its legs, and his favorite, a deer of some sort with back-curling horns. He'd sneaked up behind his father at his whittling last week and glimpsed the new shape in his lap. He knew what this beast was, a fierce lion, like the one drawn on the cover of the students' anatomy text. He yearned to hold the snarling figurine in his hands.

Christmas was the day when his parents did not work. After their meal, they would stroll along the strangely quiet canal and the ever-churning river, and turning uphill to their home, pause so the boy could slip a pretzeled chicken wing through a slot in a slave barn for one lucky captive. They would light candles against the basement's shadows, celebrating the baby god Jesus and his friend Chukwu, then climb to the roof of the college building, where his parents would spread out shards of glass and threaded shell necklaces in a glittering circle all around them and raise their arms to the winter stars, chanting words he did not understand.

Strolling down by the creek bed, he came across a little skeleton, probably a child's, picked over and clean, its bones thrown about. He lifted the domed skull, cradling it in one arm, and tapped it with a femur bone as he walked. The hollow skull thunked like a drum, that tapping beat warning off the dogs and hogs. It made him feel grand to parade amongst them in this way, sole living human within the morass, and master of all he surveyed.

LATER, he squatted in a basement corner, teasing the fattest cat with an eyeball swung on its string, the cat swiveling its head to the rhythm, yellow eyes never blinking. His father came down from the anatomy theater with a bucket and mop, having polished the tiled floor to a sheen at the end of his semester's labors. She should have been back by now, the chicken plucked and its feathers, meant for pillow stuffing, spread out drying on a gurney, lard simmering in their frying pan, and apples stewing, their sweet aroma battling the rancid gases rising from the torso on the butcher block. He needed to salt it and stash it away in the cave, or just melt it in the lye vat, wouldn't keep, though the bones might be of use.

The boy looked up, hoping for an explanation, but there was none. He plopped the eyeball into the cat's fanged mouth, and stood, asking the only important question, "Where she at, Daddy?"

They went out together, looking. The slave barns and shops were all closed, the storefronts dim. His father looked neither left nor right as he led the boy down the steep hill past the governor's mansion to the Shockoe Slip near the river, and the chicken coop out back of the grocer's shed. "Naw, she ain't come today," the grocer said, "Naw, she ain't got your chicken. Been here since sun up, busy all day, but I'd a know'd her."

The two men stood silent for a moment, as if sniffing the air for a clue, and the boy tried to mimic their stoic posture, while eyeing a jar of peppermint balls beckoning on the counter. Without another word, his father turned and walked out, the boy following, and for the rest of the afternoon they wandered, inquiring at the neighbors in their shanties along the creek. Old man Karn the cobbler pushed himself up from his rocker, shook his head sadly, and said what no one else dared on this Christmas Eve: "Steamer left this mornin' for Charleston and New Orleans, took a shipload of folks sold down that way."

Chapter 2

1860

"Flayin' a face, now, that's easy. No more'n skinnin' a rabbit, you run your blade up here at the hair line, right along there where it starts, get the whole flap, use your fingers, slide 'em in, see, peel away the forehead piece, now you try it, just tug, you might have to get up in there with your knife and snip away a thread, but come on, see how slick that is?"

"Like skinnin' a rabbit, yessuh."

The little man stood erect on a fruit crate, ready with his scalpel, in case his son erred, but proud to see the boy swallow his qualms in attempting the most gumption challenging step of the procedure. If he could do this, could leave the eyeballs in their sockets, work past the tightly gripped flesh at the nasal passages, keep the lips intact as he tugged. If he could stanch his rising gorge at the degloving of a human face, then maybe he could do this work.

In the windowless basement, the only light came from a tallow lamp, which threw shadows on the low ceiling. The dank cell smelled to high heaven, a stench unlike any other, one that clung to your clothes, got under your fingernails, and seeped up in your lungs so your own breath called to buzzards all day, a harkening not even whiskey could wash out. But the boy had been raised in these rooms, had known the stank of decaying human flesh from his first bawling breath. That part, which the prissy students found all but intolerable, meant nothing to him.

"How's that Daddy? Will that do?" The boy wouldn't grow much more, a pygmy size, everybody said. He had to reach over the body on the table, his arms braced on its breast, up close so he could have kissed the thing. He was sportin' now, showin' off. Ain't a thing bother me. And he had indeed done a fair job of it, the skin of the cheeks peeled down, the ruddy jaw muscles and the dry eyeballs on their stalks bared to the light, the whole face a rubbery mask attached now only by one strip of chin. This was a good one to start with, fresh off the gallows.

"Don't cut it off, boy, never do that. The fun of it, you'll see, slide the flap back up, fit it as good as you can there, okay? Put the face back on. Fessor Doctor come in, he'll wanna find which one of them rowdy boys keel over when he flip the flap down!"

"Yeah, I seen him do that, heh."

"Now you leave the body whole, let 'em go at that part, crack the chest, but here, you wanna split a arm down from the shoulder, both of 'em so they can come at it from both sides. He got a hunnerd boys startin' this term, we gon' be busy men."

"Yessuh, alright." Always polite, respectful, eager to learn. He'd called him a man.

The father set his scalpel aside and took ahold of the table edge to help himself down off the crate. He tried not to grunt, but his back creaked loud enough for his son to hear. Then he eased down in his rocker, pulled out a flat bottle from his apron pocket, and sucked down a draught. Which, the boy knew, would lead to a harrowing few minutes of hacking cough, living lungs more riddled and poisoned with the noxious vapors of his vocation than any dead man's. He tried to ignore it, navigated his scalpel beneath the underarm and sliced clean and shallow between the muscles there straight down to the elbow, then peeled back and pinned the paper-thin skin so the blue of the meat and the white of the nerves and tendons lay exposed like a map of a city street. No leakage at all, which was good, just starting to dry out but still pliable, the way they liked it best.

He knew why his father was teaching him all this so early, everything from stoking the coal stove to peeling a face. If he had this rare skill, could help out around the college, then maybe they wouldn't sell him away when he came of age. His eyes went blurry, so he had to pull back the scalpel and lean on an elbow for a minute. His father might think it was the fumes, but really it was the dawning realization that the day would come when the man he most loved, practically the only real man he'd ever known, would end up like this sack of meat and bones. Along with that horror, too, the fear that some body snatcher would dig him up and commit just such an indignity on his helpless corpse. Not on my watch, he promised himself, not this.

CHAPTER 3

1863

BILLIE BAKER'S refuge on the far edge of Poor House Hill for years now had been a hole at the rotting base of an ancient sycamore tree that he just fit into with his legs sticking out. He backed into the cool of the hollow and allowed himself the only rest he'd have all day. Now to be tree tall, he thought, to stretch up towards the clouds and see clear to the river, with memories back across the old tree's two hundred years to the Powhatans picking mussels in the shallows, and the first English boats paddling upriver to no good. He never knew if the putrid odor out here was some grave uncovered by dog packs or diggers or more likely, he guessed, just the fumes off his coat, but he discerned a milder fragrance, too, sometimes a rose bouquet, mingled with the sharp aroma from the tobacco barns on the river, the ripe fog from the nearby tannery, and the wood smoke from the city's chimneys, all the different decaying, burning, rotting scents that a city turned up all over again every day. That reek settled down along the creekbed and hung in the brambles, so thick you could almost part it with your hand.

His boy Chris would be along, he'd be able to find the tall, bone white tree even at midnight, leading the two poor boys in this year's class. It was a damaged haul, they wouldn't know for sure until they got them back to the basement, but the grave digger had said he'd left three Union soldier boys shallow and stacked, easy pickings. Couldn't use the ambulance this time. City on starvation rations, so the Fessor Doctor had sold off the dray horse for three bushels of corn. Chris would bring the barrow, the shovels, the tarp. The students would bring their promise to dig for a dime. Billie had his pistol and his will to use it. Now he just needed to wait under the tree as the old ones scattered gems across the purpling sky and a lone barn owl awoke with a chortle to its own night of savage hunting. This was his favorite time, always, out alone in the early Spring air, nothing to do. Though waiting too was a side of the work, work that was all day and night if you did it right. Out here for a few he could let his eyelids shutter, hidden in the shelter of the tortured old tree, and see where his dreams might wander.

And how they wandered, too, but after all they had so much to work with. If he reached out his calloused and salt bleached hand at arm's length, so his palm covered the college building that was his home on the next hill, Billie's whole nightmarish world fit in the stretch of his stubby fingers. At his pointer the slave barns, a stone's throw down the hill, still thriving in the midst of war, where they'd dump the bodies sometimes not even dead yet, spasming from the dropsy or a cane to the head, out the back door with the slop and the offal and a wink, knowing old Billie would be along to drag them off before they stiffened. At his little finger, the far reach of his domain, lay the prison camp on Belle Isle, where any day you could pick among a dozen corpses so starved that lye dissolved them down to bone in an hour, a good haul if they were studying skeletons that week. Along the river and his palm, at the turning basin, it was the working ladies. If you needed a female you could find them there. The mattress girls who'd throw down right on the canal bank, but, of course, not a one would stoop so low as to reconnoiter with the ghoul of the city. He'd walk the river in the hours before dawn and like as not somebody'd got smart, somebody'd got cut or throttled, and nobody ever said a word.

There at his ring finger lay the Foundling Hospital, where the mangled half-born were left aswaddle, if he could reach them before the dog packs that roamed the streets like a cavalry. Up close the alms house loomed, filled to the brim these days with war wounded, the dead piled out back in an open shed, awaiting some kind of burial. At his middle finger stood the prison gallows, busier than ever now. The Capitol Building hid there, too, on the other side of his hand, its churchy white walls all proud and fancy. That was the real killing floor, of course, the Confederate Congress in their dandy suits whipping the war along.

So yes he could dream. He dreamed the dead dancing. He dreamed them waltzing full fleshed in hoop skirts and dress grays with bloody grinning skulls. He dreamed them melting in the lye vat and unmelting again to climb out and slap him flathanded in the face. He dreamed them driving locomotives and poling barges and staving in each other's pumpkin soft heads with cudgels. Sometimes he dreamed them fucking. He had a lot to dream, but however fantastic, none of his dreams matched his waking life, the job of work he knew so well, and damned if he'd give it up now.

Except that one, a vision, really. The monster that had swirled up from a long time back, ebbing and flowing in its wonders, adding and subtracting its terrors, so the whole extravaganza flowed across his sleeping mind like the James in torrent after storms, those nights before they'd built the Medical College and dug the pit he'd requested, when he'd wrap up what was left, slough and nubbins, bundle it all in a canvas tarp, and haul it dripping down his back in the darkest hours out onto the Mayo Bridge to disgorge unrecognizable slubs of flesh into the rapids below. If a late student was about, maybe a few playing cards, he'd say he was headed out to "feed the river."

And maybe that was his mistake, what pissed the river off. Because when his pipe drooped and his eyes closed in a cat nap sometimes that river would swirl into his sleep, foam up, take on a devilish shape, many-armed, and dance some stomping campfire jig, a ring of bloody skulls for a belt, and of late, this new scene in the dream, his eyeball bucket would spring up, too, eyeballs trailing their stringy stalks crawling up onto the headless beast, forming a writhing mass of eyes that sees you any direction you run, the skulls on the belt just uproarious in their laughter as the many hands reached and grabbed and wrestled each other for their prize.

This dream had worried him so, he even acknowledged it when the Fessor Doctor caught him dozing in his rocker one afternoon. Another doctor from up north, town called Cambridge, they said, holding a finger to his nose and speaking in that queer northern accent, had counseled, "Yes, our nightmares, my boy, can torment us. But do this, if you turn and face the demon, do not run. Stand bold and face it in your dream. I believe if you do, it will strengthen your waking resolve in all your daily tests."

Billie had stood up quick, embarrassed, licking away spittle at his lips. He'd shown the visitor around the basement, demonstrating the lift to the dissection room with its crank table and side troughs, the lye vat, empty of bones on that particular day, the pit dug wide by two men with shovels standing back-to-back 30 feet deeper in the river silt where the last of it went, saving him that walk to the Mayo Bridge of late. The cabinet of saws, scissors, scalpels, hammers, chisels and specimen trays. The mercury and other specialty draughts. The pickling jars stuffed with still-born monstrosities, some no bigger than potatoes. And damned if that doctor hadn't admired it all, said it beat his set up at his northern school, called it Harvard College, and that he'd take back what he'd learned and try it there. The Fessor Doctor had touched old Billie then, maybe for the first time in his life with his bare hand, laid a manicured hand on his shoulder, and said he was proud of his work.

The northern doctor inquired then on what he called "the acquisition of materiel," pronouncing that last word funny, like he was French or something. Up his way, his diggers had a whole big city, too, to pull from, that free town Boston, but the constables were such a trouble, you could never tell who to pay now or how much, and the citizenry would not tolerate the sight of an opened grave. Just last year an anatomy riot, when ambitious resurrectionists, he called them, tore up the decorous and beautifully landscaped St. Auburn Cemetery, snatching a white minister's own son.

The Fessor Doctor scoffed at that. "We have none of those difficulties here." He did not have to explain why that was. The young doctor, who had, of course, walked past the many slave traders' stalls on his way up from the train, admired the unstated logistics in Richmond, then asked, "Your materiel, would I assume that it is largely negroid in its constitution?"

"You would, for the most part, yes. Their bodies are so much more readily available than the hairy apes, and close enough, shall we say, to use for practice."

"Well sir, they are men, are they not?"

"As you say, of course."

The visitor then wondered if some commerce could be arranged, a transport of skeletons, at least, by rail or sail. The Fessor Doctor nodded towards Billie, who responded, "Yessuh, 'xpect we can pack some up for you in some brine in a barrel, 'bout anything you need."

"We shall discuss terms in my office, then," the Fessor Doctor said. "Billie, your offer is to our honor."

The northern doctor lifted a bone saw from the wall, curved like a scimitar, and well-balanced with gleaming teeth. "Have you a sawyer from whom we might procure such instruments?" he asked.

"Indeed, within a mile of this college we have anything an anatomist might desire – barrel stavers, bladesmiths, cutlers, smithies, whiskey stills, all manner of necessary chemicals from salt to quicklime, and for materiel, as you say, well you can see for yourself, from the *peculiarity* of our institutions, cadavers for dissection can be obtained in abundance, and we believe their availability is not surpassed by any city in our troubled land. Yes, my friend, I am sure we can supply your needs and our own to your fancy."

The northern doctor replaced the saw on the wall, then sneezed into a handkerchief scented with lavender so heavily that Billie could smell it from across the room. "By the by, sir, have you heard from Brown-Sequard?"

"Oh my," the Fessor Doctor frowned, "We had hoped never again to hear that name."

"I believe he's off to Paris, last I heard."

"To China for all I care! My god, man, if you'd seen the menagerie he made of this place!"

"Something of a vivisectionist, was he?"

Billie took up a broom and began sweeping a corner of the basement at that name, afraid he'd speak unless distracted. That lunatic, making the students round up cats and dogs all over the city, trap raccoons and possums at the dumps, kept them all in the basement in one steel cage together, right next to Billie's living quarters. The rowl and racket, cats eating the possums, dogs eating the cats, then going after each other, all night and day. Billie and his wife with a toddler still in a gown, trying to raise him up in such an infernal mess.

"I suppose you may have heard of his nearly mortal experiment investigating the perspiration function," the Fessor Doctor was saying.

"Yes, that story has made the rounds, I'm afraid, a cautionary tale for the rest of us, wouldn't you say?" the visitor replied.

"I can't imagine anyone else addled enough to attempt such a feat."

"No, I should hope not."

The two doctors disappeared up the stairs as they chatted, leaving Billie with his memories of that year, when he had been ordered to strap living animals onto the carving table, where they struggled and wailed against that mad professor's experiments. He cut into their bellies, sucked out stomach juice with a syringe, even tasted the stuff and passed it around to show the students how acidic it was. He skinned the poor beasts alive and carved into their spines to demonstrate the causes of paralysis. But to their credit, the animals fought back. One cur bit through the professor's hand and a cat – the cats fought hardest, wouldn't have none of his shenanigans – jumped on his head before he could strap it down and nearly tore out his eyes.

Then that one day, Billie heard a bump upstairs over all the bawling in the cage and went up to find old Brown-Sequard flat out on the floor of the anatomy arena, not a stitch on him, and shiny as a bronze statue. Billie thought at first he'd died. But what he'd done, he'd got a bucket of wood varnish and painted himself all over with it, like he was tired of being white, and when the shellac hardened, he'd sealed himself up tight and couldn't move.

"What that fool doctor done now?" Billie spoke aloud. Behind him, the little boy stood watching. It was his earliest memory, seeing his father race downstairs for rubbing alcohol and sand paper, get to scrubbing the frozen doctor on the floor, sweat pouring off of him as he worked on his hands and knees, until at last the man stirred, and downstairs all the while the squabbling animals. The best part of the memory, though, was that pointed question his father had asked. He'd had opportunities enough for that one himself.

And then it was over. The mad professor put on his clothes, freed what animals were left out into the street, and never returned to the college building, no doubt from the shame of it. Or the Board of Visitors had finally had enough. Can't run a medical school cutting on animals. You got to have human bodies for that these days. And the new Fessor Doctor, he could carve a corpse down to bone in a week when he got going. Though most of the time he left that up to his demonstrator assistant, or Billie, of course, who knew his way around a rib cage and pelvis as keen as the sharpest butcher on Cary Street.

"Funny, people don't like their graves disturbed," the demonstrator had laughed, "but whatever you do, don't go stealing their hunting dogs!" They might have let him get away with shellacking himself, but when the governor's English pointer went missing, well old Brown-Sequard had to go.

Later, the Fessor Doctor came down again and asked, "Do you know who that was?" A big shot to the mind of the white folk, philosopher, he said. Anatomy doctor, famous person up north. Billie tried the man's trick, too, and damned if it didn't work! Next time the river rose up, turned that grasping eyeball livid monster on him, he stood firm on his dream bridge midstream and even dared to reach out a trembling hand in welcome. How them skulls along the belt line cackled over that! But then the thing turned all its roving eyes on him, shrank down to his size, and together they patrolled the city that night. In his dream, every soul they crossed fell stone dead at their feet.

The beast's many arms grabbed the bodies up and into its gaping belly maw they went.

Whether any of that nightmare courage helped him in his waking hours, Billie couldn't say. Wasn't much he feared anyway, had seen just about everything evil a man could do in the conscripted rounds of his neighborhood, and knew how to hold his own. His wife lost to the slavers, he was certain. He should have gone with her to get that chicken, could have saved the laboratory cleanup from end of term for another day. They'd kidnapped her, sold her South most likely, gone on that steamer like she'd never lived at all. Sometimes he imagined she'd come back, or wanted to strike out after her, but thinking like that was only another way to let your head go soft. The Fessor Doctor at the time, he'd offered to ask around – she had been the college's property after all – but nothing ever came of that.

Billie lit his pipe, adding the rich scent of burley to the evening fog, and gazed out past his boots to the muddy lawn of the cemetery. Nobody put up gravestones here, these were poor people, no names, and those enslaved, free for the taking, but you had to act quick. Most interred without a coffin, wrapped in a sheet, ready food for the worms and laid shallow so sometimes the dogs would beat him to it.

Illegal, of course, but the real risk wasn't the constables, who had other worries in this wartime town. It was the competition, the out-of-town diggers from that college in Charlottesville, and the free lancers working for a bottle. He fingered the gun at his waist. Had not fired it once in anger, understanding if a white man knew he had it, he'd be whipped or hanged, Fessor Doctor or no, but if he had to, yes, he'd make it known.

He sensed a rain brewing upriver. The cemetery mud would soften to pudding, the looming clouds a cloak and the sleety showers shooing the police, if there were any about, inside to some late-night tavern. A promising outing indeed, and here came young Chris with his barrow, bent to his work up the hill, a cracked mirror image of old Billie himself. He set into coughing, so the boy cocked his head and nodded, adjusting his route towards the tree. He'll take up this work when I'm gone, he thought. He sees what's in it. Like I tell him, you do what you have to. Some people, and this is rare, do the thing they're good at. And if it's something no one else can do. More especially, if it's something no one else *will* do, then however this war turns out, you a free man then for sure.

CHAPTER 4

APRIL 3, 1865

BILLIE HAD PREPARED TO RUN, if the generals decided to burn the college building. But that was the safest place in the end, since wounded soldiers packed the infirmary upstairs. They hung yellow bed sheets out the windows, leaving the invalids and amputees to the Yankees, when they cleared on off down South. Billie and his son holed up in the basement, dinner of corn bread and dandelion salad in the dark, careful not to show a sign or make a peep, while the city went to hell around them.

Chris awoke with a keening hum in his ears, a gift of night-long staccato explosions as fire swept the city. He followed his father up from the basement and took his hand to step out between the paired columns of the college building, twin gnomes in black overcoats, surveying what looked like the end of the world. Only a few structures remained untouched, the churches up here along the Broad Street ridge, the soot-smudged Capitol down the hill a bit, and the looming college building where they stood. The rest of the city all the way to the river—just a smoking rubble.

But what really struck Chris, wandering before them in the street, came a rabble of barely clothed men and women and children. Looking about, bewildered, searching, mumbling to each other. One man naked to the world covered himself with a hand but came up the steps and asked if it was true. Billie suppressed a look of disdain, but caught himself in the torrent of change, then dropped Chris' hand, unbuttoned his coat and with a gallant gesture helped the other man on with it.

Billie said, "Yeah, I believe we done with all that. We free now, for sure, brother. You go on."

Chris gazed at the bedraggled figures of the freedmen straggling away down Marshall Street. He asked, "What will become of them, Daddy?"

"Bird build a nest, rabbit find a hole, people make a way," he guessed.

"Do you think Mama?"

"Go get the pick-axe, boy."

Chris followed his father down the debris-strewn hill behind the be-sooted governor's mansion to the slave trader's row along Wall Street. At the first storefront they reached, the door stood open, its plate glass window shattered. They stepped gingerly on the crunching glass, made their way past the office desks and the show parlor to the stable door in back. Billie lifted a heavy oak door-bar, then told Chris to go at the padlock with his pick-axe. He stepped back as Chris went to work, the boy's third swing knocking the bolt from the door.

The stench that hit them when they slid the door open easily matched that of their basement rooms in the college. One stripe of sunlight from a crack in the wall sliced the darkness. Billie went back to the office and returned with an oil lantern and flint striker, the lamplight revealing six bodies leaning together at the center of the stall as if to hold each other up, their hands tied, and a commotion about their heads that made Chris recoil, a troop of rats feasting at the bowls of their caved in skulls.

The next two stables were empty, desks overturned and

papers scattered about. Perhaps the slavers had herded their captives elsewhere, or in a fleeting moment of desperate compassion, opened the doors and run. But people lurked blinking in other stables, so that eventually Billie and Chris led a parade of freedmen, who foraged in the clothes chests and chiffarobes of the display rooms, emerging in petticoats, ragged knee breeches, or wrapped in drapes. At the foot of the street, warehouses smoldered, black smoke mingled with the fires from the nearby foundries and a ripe aroma of burned flesh drifted in the settling ashes. They headed back up the street, checking at each of the abandoned slaving stores, their party growing, until they reached the largest establishment, Lumpkins Jail, its tall barn doors thrown open. How often Billie had retrieved corpses from the drainage ditch there to supply the college's anatomy classes, sometimes two or three a week. But on this morning, the usually bustling site of human commerce lay empty, abandoned, its occupants long dispersed.

Billie handed the oil lamp to the nearest of his followers, lit it, and waved for him to toss it inside. But the man knew better. This lantern was his first possession, a real prize. He blew out the flame, cradled the fragile glass globe in his arms, and turned away. As Chris remembered it, across that whole impossible morning no one of their crew had spoken a word. To the end of his life he'd wonder if he'd only dreamt it all.

That afternoon, Billie and Chris wandered, touching nothing, just taking in the ruins. Factory floors accordioned down on themselves. A single wall of a warehouse tottering in the haze. A mighty locomotive melted like wax down onto its tracks. A monstrous tangle of metal a block long that had been a printing press. Cannon balls scattered like marbles all down Tredegar Hill. No way to cross the river, blown bridges smoking in the dead calm of that April day, and staved in barges cluttering the turning basin.

Here and there, gangs of white men in blue slacks battled warehouse fires, but the only other people along their way sat numb in the rubble. In the background, all day long, the city made a rumbling noise like it was groaning.

———————

THEY SLEPT as they always had, on the floor pallet in the basement, nowhere else to go. Billie lay restless beside the sleeping boy, staring into the darkness, because the truth of it, he guessed, was that they could in fact go anywhere. In the morning, he fed the boy the last of their biscuits, set a rat trap for their evening meal, and melted down the corpse of an old woman, dry as leather, he'd brought in from the asylum for the term's final dissection lab. No message had come, but he surmised correctly that the Fessor Doctor had canceled all classes.

They were standing again at the top of the stairs, between the college building's squat columns, when the American President's entourage passed by. Chris noted how the white boy in his pretty bow tie held his gawky father's hand as they led a straggling procession of freedmen up the street to what the Fessor Doctor called the White House on the corner. The tall, bearded father paused before the college building, as if to admire its queer Egyptian-modeled architecture, then tipped his top hat to Billie and Chris. Billie wore no hat, but nodded in reply. Chris dared to wave his hand, and the boy in the bow tie waved back.

They spent the rest of the day indoors, occupied by the routine end of school year mopping, made more tedious by all the ash that had sifted in from the fires. They shared a pan-fried rat, then climbed up to the roof and looked about. Crowds mingled at Monument Church on the next block and at the First African Baptist Church nearby. Thumping music from a marching band echoed along Broad Street. Most of the fires were out by then, the smoke had cleared away, and sunset painted high streaked clouds in candy colors. Before the sky could darken, a full moon rose orange above the Union soldiers' wagon train straggling down from Church Hill. Out there beyond the river, at some immeasurable distance, it was just possible that she might be gazing at this same moonrise. Billie had never let himself hope, had considered the cause entirely lost, but in a day the world had turned upside down, so maybe.

He offered the boy a bag of shiny pebbles and showed him how to arrange them in a circle at their feet. Then he raised his arms and chanted to the darkening sky. Chris hooked his fingers around his father's belt, fearing the man might lift from the roof and fly away.

CHAPTER 5

AUGUST 1865

CHRIS HAD SEEN the doctors do a lot of odd things, but this was a new one. He crouched near the top of the stairs, and watched in wonder, his father perched where he had never dared sit before, in a pew of the dissecting theatre, but stranger than that, the Fessor Doctor himself also sat in the pew, just an arm's reach away. The Fessor Doctor was speaking quietly, but with that deep-chested voice of command Chris knew so well. Had his father been a mule, he'd have used the same tone of voice, no doubt expecting his janitor to understand only half of what was said.

Chris heard it all.

"Our circumstances have changed, here Billie, as have yours, of course. We would not blame you if you chose to go, if you left to seek out your dear wife, wherever she may be."

Chris' father said nothing. He sat erect in the pew, eyes set on the bare dissecting table in the middle of the theater, giving no sign that he had heard the Fessor Doctor at all. Chris watched and learned, admiring how his father stiffened himself against displaying any hint of deference or satisfaction. Perhaps this was what emancipation meant, a precarious rebalancing, a disorienting shift in manners. So far, in this building, nothing had changed that he could see.

The Fessor Doctor seemed unaware of all that, but he did appreciate that something must be done to keep this man, this indispensable laborer, at his beck and call. Across the city beds went unmade, breakfasts unserved, horses unshod, clothes unwashed, as every day more of the newly freed simply walked away from their former owners, like sheep unfenced, he thought, to other places, other opportunities, anywhere but here. If the college was to rebuild, was to launch a full year of medical training again, they would need cadavers, weekly all through the colder months. The Fessor Doctor's wife had attempted baking a loaf of bread, but breaking into graves, haunting the back door of the alms house, taking hanged men down from the gallows, this was more than he could imagine ever doing himself.

He said, "You know, Billie, we did send out missives, emissaries, seeking your wife. We looked for her. Nothing turned up at all. If, as you suspect, she was kidnapped south, then yes, I understand that you would want to search for her. But the land is broad, across several states. You could not walk its breadth in a year. Your wife knows this place, she knows you are here, and her son. Would it not be more sensible to wait in a place she knows, that she can find, and come to, when she is able? Imagine you out and on the road somewhere, she returning, and you not here?"

Chris sank onto the steps, confused. Billie had said nothing to him about going in search of his mother. It seemed impossible to imagine finding her, if indeed she was still alive. What was the Fessor Doctor saying?

His father sat still as a corpse, no hint of feeling in his expression, except a tightening at the jaw. If the Fessor Doctor noticed the risk he skirted, he seemed willing to dare it. He continued, "Well, this, Billie. What we can offer. A salary of five dollars a month, your room and fire wood, as now, with your son. And for each item of anatomy materiel you bring, complete bodies only, two dollars paid in Union bills that very week. You are a freedman now, of course, can take or leave my offer, but I daresay none better will come your way. What say you, then?"

"If it was your wife, suh, what would you do?" Chris' jaw dropped in amazement at that. His father had just compared his situation to this white man's and to his face at that. And equally amazing, the Fessor Doctor took it calmly, as if the idea made sense.

He said, "I hope that I would go and stop at nothing until we were reunited in each others' arms." The words came out liltingly, the way you would sing a song.

"Then I'ma stay," Billie replied, putting an end to that foolishness.

The Fessor Doctor sputtered and took out a handkerchief to wipe his forehead. "You will stay?"

"But it go you don't pay me sometime, we gone."

"Yes, of course we shall pay you, a freedman, after all."

"This all start today, then?" Billie asked, his eyes drilling the dissection table.

"Your salary monthly all year, half that amount when college is not in session. You keep the facilities in order at all times, as always, in that nothing changes. Only this agreement is new."

"Well then."

"You will stay?"

"You pay like you say."

The Fessor Doctor stood then, even made a sort of half bow. "On behalf of the faculty, Billie, we thank you."

Chris would never forget his father's response, stunning in its boldness. He made no reply, allowing only the slightest acknowledging nod.

The Interview

"Am I correct," the reporter asked, settling into his chair with notepad at the ready, *"That you were born in this building, enslaved?"*

"First thing I know'd is right here," Baker replied, pulling a clay pipe from his vest pocket.

"And upon Emancipation, you chose to stay on?"

"Daddy did and I stayed with him."

"Did you ever think to strike out elsewhere? A different life?"

"Oh yeah, still do, now you ask."

"Yet you remain here, janitor, diener, anatomy assistant."

"Here I sit."

"I mean, you live among the dead, man. These chemicals, poisons, the stench of decay. For so many years, the risk of arrest in the cemeteries. Your people shun you."

"Shoot me, too."

"What is it, then, Chris? What is the attraction, after all?"

Tamping tobacco into his pipe, Baker allowed a sly grin. "Come down the basement, you try it sometime. Never know. Might catch your fancy, too."

CHAPTER 6

FEBRUARY 1866

CHRIS LURKED at the corner of 3rd and Leigh Streets watching the students at play. In the street, girls spun so their dresses unfurled or held their skirts close as their feet danced to the jump rope, chanting a sing-song tune with the rope's swirling rhythm. Boys crouched at the curb shooting jacks. School was legal now for Negroes, but not for this one. He already a working man. He could spell, could read some words, could count his fingers and toes. The rest you pick up on your own.

Being out on the street had never been fun. The punches, the kicks, the rocks to the noggin, the taunts, the shaming, because of what his daddy did, because of where they lived, in that towering, tapered box with the stubby columns out front, where who knew what went on. He'd learned enough, how to crouch, tuck his head in his coat collar, run. The words were just words, the bruises healed, but it was a lonely way. He waited until the teacher rang her bell and the kids all lined up to get swallowed into their lessons, then turned to make his rounds, to see what mishaps might have befallen the night laborers.

Chris draped his burlap sack across one shoulder and launched downhill to the river, navigating the slippery cobblestones and dodging the rickety farm wagons pulled by surly mules that had trudged in all night from the country. At the foot of the hill, he waited for the Lynchburg day train to clear the tracks, its coal smoke belching high on this chilly winter day and mingling with the billow from all the factory smokestacks along the river. Pale ladies at the train windows upturned their fur collars, icy slop spattered in the alleys, bums sprawled in the muck, canal workers rolled barrels down the middle of the street, and lawmakers in capes jumped puddles, the entire river-front a jumbled rumbling carnival. He'd been watching them rebuild, almost a miracle to see how fast it could transpire, the whole city down from the Medical College building and the Capitol emerging brick by brick from rubble.

And now look at it, already the waterfront thriving, maybe more than ever, really. Some of those freedmen folks had walked straight out of the Wall Street slave stalls and built a neighbor-hood for themselves up the hill. Trains unloading coal and tobacco and safes and sofas, the islands on the river sprouting tent cities teeming with new arrivals from points south, and the college expanding from a four-month war-time term, aimed only at showing a boy how to amputate, up to its old two-year diploma. So they needed flesh to cut on.

Which is where Chris headed now. In the alley behind every factory and mill he turned over the yellow bucket stashed high on a ledge to deter the dogs. He reached in for whatever the night may have wrought, severed hands, fingers, feet, on occa-sion a shredded arm. Black parts, white parts, all a mingle, and none of that mattered to Chris. He dropped them into his tote, moved on to the next place, and by noon most days had a haul. He trudged up the hill again and spilled it all out on the anatomy table for his father to sort through.

People ignored him, he had found, on his way down the hill. But on the way back up, gunny dripping, they avoided his eyes, made occult gestures with their hands, cursed and crossed to the other side of the street. Sometimes he caught a rock to the side of the head. So of late he'd made up a turban stuffed with wool that he donned even on warmer days. Made him look foreign, maybe a little priestly in an Asian kind of way, and when he disappeared between the stolid columns of that Egyptian looking college building, it all made a kind of awkward sense, amidst the fantastic tumult of the rebuilding city, the medical school's young pariah on the prowl.

CHAPTER 7

MAY 31, 1867

HOLLYWOOD CEMETERY SPREAD across a choice hilltop at the edge of town, with eastward views of the riverfront and its bustling industry, though far enough away to avoid the choking factory fumes, the clang of the steel mill, the horse flop squishy streets and the bustling trains. White ladies with parasols strolled the grounds, taking their health, laying wreaths, consorting with the youthful dead who yet seemed just two years since to reside in that thin place between here and what people called the beyond.

Much to be done, but Billie had to see this. He tied a cravat about his neck, and helped his son do the same, then they strode among the other citizens to the hillside. Coffins had been arriving for months, from as nearby as Cold Harbor and Petersburg and from as far as Tennessee and Mississippi, boxes of bones dug up from the hastily filled battlefield graveyards of the war and from family plots on ruined farms, name and rank carved into the pine lids, and all the boxes stacked high on wagons pulled by mules up from the railway yard to the cemetery's imposing stone gates. The Fessor Doctor had ended the term early, to free Billie and Chris to what he called a noble task, helping with the digging.

Billie had taken charge of one section, specialist in this work that he was. He drew chalk lines on the meadow, and lay tarp for neat piles of dirt at the side of each open grave. For thirty days he oversaw the digging of twenty Black workers loaned out from a tobacco mill. Chris put his back to the work, too. Now, on the day of consecration, he thought if anyone owned this event, it was these diggers. Someone said they'd buried 7,000 Confederate dead here. It might have been a million. The work crews had worn down dozens of shovels in the effort. Though on this day, when the white ladies stepped down from their horse-drawn carriages, burdened by sprays of flowers that had them looking like walking gardens, and made their way along the winding promenades, the men who'd done all the digging were kept outside the gates.

At the edge of the cemetery, in any case, Black burghers gathered. A baking hot day, at the cusp of summer, the faintest breeze whispering on this lovely hill. The diggers, like Billie and his boy dressed for this marvel in their Sunday suits, doffed their hats and stood silent on the periphery. There would be time later, for decades, to recount what they had observed on this last day of May, to chuckle in the barber shops, to sing it in verse, but you had to be there to see it first, all that planed pine wood and half penny nails put to this good use, securing the mealy bones of all those boys who'd died to keep them in chains.

At the northern corner of the cemetery, graves from the early Virginia battles — Bull Run, Fredericksburg, Seven Days — had already flattened and gone green as a lawn. Towards the river the more recently buried lay under soft piles of tamped dirt in row after row across the swales, then finally down here close to where the Black folk gathered, the outer ring of the dead were going in today. Mule wagons pulled in at the gate, one by one, and only those diggers required for this solemn celebration were allowed in to do the work. They wore white cotton shirts, hefted gleaming new shovels, and moved without speaking or raising their heads, putting the last of these rebel stiffs in the ground once and for all.

The white ladies fanned their faces, sobbed beneath their parasols, and shifted wreaths of roses in their arms. A few went down in a faint and were carted off to a shade tree to recover. The gimpy men from the Veterans' Home and a few proud old officers stood in ranks in moth-frayed gray uniforms, jaws set, as a band blared dirges that drowned out whatever the graveside ministers might have been praying. It all seemed to take forever.

Billie and his son Chris stood off to the side in the shade of the chapel. He'd supervised the digging, disbursed pay chits with his own hands, but the minute that transaction was completed, he and his boy became again what they'd been before, grave robbers, body snatchers, and outcasts. No one even nodded their way.

Billie found a wooden crate and took a seat. Months of digging up here on the hill had tired him tremendously. Up all day shoveling and giving orders in this white man's graveyard, up all night prowling the pauper's field and hauling fresh stiffs to the college, had hit him hard. Standing up straight and sitting both hurt about the same. Sometimes it was like a phantom hand rose up and choked off his breath. No, he wasn't right, that was for sure.

Hollywood was a fine cemetery, like none Chris had ever seen. To him, a whole lot of celebration and hoo ha over boxes full of bones. But that's how people were these days, his father had said, treating the dead with more care than the living. Well, some dead anyway. Chris knew that tonight, on the slope of Poor House Hill, he'd be digging again. A boat waving a quarantine flag had arrived from South America, disgorged its guano and its dead, and the Fessor Doctor needed two corpses boiled down to bone and wired up as display skeletons for friends on his summer Grand Tour of Europe. Up here it was rose garlands and winding paved paths and a man would be a fool to mess with these graves the way the white folk prayed and swooned over them. It was the lost boys, no name or address, that he needed. And there was always more of them.

Chapter 8

1868

"It's different now, Daddy, you a paid man. They ain't throw you out. And that's why I'm here anyway, to help out."

"It's my leg, won't do right."

"I seen it. You lay up now, I can do it."

"But the new students comin'. You got to get them lined up or they run all over you."

"It's just a greetin'. I tell the Fessor Doctor you out scoutin', he be good with that."

"He come down here, see me you say that, we both be on the street."

"Daddy, who else know what we know? What he gon' do?"

No that's where you're wrong, don't ever think that way, Billie wanted to say, though he had spent his entire life here at the college constructing just such a bulwark against their whims. If he had been upright, he might have slapped the boy. Instead, he lifted himself on an elbow, tried to push himself up from the floor pallet, then fell back. Getting on towards dawn, work to do. "You go," he sighed. "I be on when I can."

Chris set a bowl of hot meal and a tin cup of water at his father's side. "You want your pipe?" he asked.

"Man don't smoke in bed, that's a rule."

"Be right outside the door."

Billie squinted up at the boy looming above him in his leather apron and black coat, hair newly trimmed for the upcoming term, face scrubbed and shining in lantern light, blank eyes of a child seen too much. Every day more like he was in his own youth, compact package, head on a swivel, eager to make his way. But the difference now, this liberation, he could up and go any day, point his feet any direction, maybe find his mama, make a life out of something other than death if he cared to. But here the boy stood, same as always, never no sign of an itch.

Chris nodded and turned, closing the door to leave his father abed in the dark. Across his entire life, Billie had never laid in, feared the lure of it now. Maybe just a minute, he thought. Get up before the students arrive. His old river companion roiled up then, practically filling the room, glowing belly skulls laughing at that and eyes ogling around on their bloody stalks like they needed a stretch. *You ain't need to move*, the monster said, *we can wander all we want right here.* Billie lay back, the familiar rank stench from Chris stirring bones in the lye vat seeping under the door. Boy could handle it, he guessed that he could. *Come now*, said the nightmare creature, beckoning with all his beefy hands, *got somethin' you wanna see.*

———

CHRIS STOOD ready when the students arrived, at the cutting table upstairs in the anatomy arena under the skylight, hands clasped at his back, alert as a butler, his demeanor a balance of deference and command. This first day they wore vested suits and polished boots, ten of them in all, big-eared, gangly, sniffing at the malodorous air. He meant nothing to them yet, he knew.

They were sizing each other up, ranking status, stiff and nervous, clocking the gleaming empty carving tables.

Chris knew them at a glance. Three with that easy poise, raised up on the plantation ruins, second sons who could ride, but nothing for them now on the broken farms. Four city boys, in the ribbon ties they wore these days, already slouching, feigning familiarity with this Egyptian temple they'd never been in, though it had loomed at the end of Marshall Street their whole lives. Three poor boys, too, up from the country like as not, holes in their bootsoles, sons of the scavengers who were rebuilding the city a brick at a time. They'd be his diggers, would need the pay. Would break them in easy like his father always said.

The Fessor Doctor swept in without ceremony, strode briskly among the students, but paused to shake their hands with an appraising look behind his thick spectacles. Ten white boys raised up in a ruined world, hoping perhaps to help it mend. The Fessor Doctor went to the podium and bade the boys to take a seat in the gallery around. Chris stood right where he was. Man cleared his throat, ran a hand through his silvery mane of hair, and spoke without paper right off the top of his head. Same sermon every year, had it memorized good. He started right in with the high calling, inviting these boys to step up to the knife, to learn what modern doctoring was all about. That familiar line that still gave Chris a little thrill, because he knew it to be true and it was said so well: "The scalpel is the highest power to which you can appeal. Its revelations are beyond the reach of the cavils and the various opinions of men.

"This right here is what makes a doctor," he told them, "what separates your work from the charlatan fare of the faith healers, the medicine show carnies, the elixir men, the midwives, the barbers. Yes, we dare to inspect the body, inside and out."

And here came the best phrase: "Poets," he intoned, "speak of the heart like it's some winged Cupid with a bow. But you will hold a human heart in your hand, feel its heft, admire its weave of hoses, see that a heart is but a muscle, though a mighty one, that it pumps a nourishing flood coursing to your toes to water its garden, your flesh, from your first bawling cry to your last choking gasp in old age. And that tireless fist pumping behind your cage of ribs, I would submit, outstrips in its eloquence any sonnet ever written. This atrium, young men, is your courtroom, where the corporeal states its case. We who wear the cognomen *doctor*, we own the flesh and bone. As my own instructor, the illustrious Xavier Bichet himself taught, 'Open up a few corpses, you will dissipate at once the darkness.' And so you shall, young men, so you shall."

At that he bent to a crate at his side and called the students up one-by-one, reciting their full names, middle names, too, like they were graduating or something. They came forward to receive a fat book, the bible of anatomy that would teach them the ropes. Though Chris knew already which five of the ten wouldn't crack a spine of their texts all year. That was what he and his father were for. Bring up the bodies, break out the saws. The great draw of this school was that here you learned by doing.

At a nod from the podium Chris then pulled out his satchel and with a little flourish opened it on a towel spread across the carving table. He took out scalpels and tweezers and wrapped them in pairs in handkerchiefs, then offered a bundle to each of the boys. For the first time he spoke, surprising himself with the authority in his voice, parroting his father's words, "These are your tools and you keep 'em safe and sharp. Every surgeon has 'em, like a carpenter has his."

The Fessor Doctor added, "Indeed, gentlemen. Your scalpel

can reveal the most beautiful and profound structures of the body, its intricate and noble fabric. We men of medicine do not fear the knife. We pierce to the core of the human frame, unsheathe the mystery over which our skin is but a thin veneer, and reveal the truer miracle, the pulleys, the bellows, what a poet has called the body electric. Dissection, gentlemen, is the basis of surgery. The work you do in this operating theatre shall inform your minds, guide your hands, and familiarize your hearts to what is required of a modern physician. This practice will season you to the work, will steel you to a kind of *necessary inhumanity*."

Chris shifted his feet, a little impatient. How that man loved the sound of his voice.

"We must turn the cadaver into a three-dimensional text-book, a limited edition, if you will, of tissues and organs," the Fessor Doctor continued. "Without your scalpel, without this course of study, you would be but a huckster, a charlatan, a quack. When you have completed your terms inside these walls, you will have joined a fraternity of scientists, of artists, too, who dare to grapple with the marvelous truth of our very being. And with that knowledge, young men, you shall heal."

The students received the holy bundles solemnly, eyeing the gleaming carving tables and the squat black man with his stern composure who dared to return their gaze. Some felt their first thrilled qualms at what they had signed up for. Chris and the Fessor Doctor scanned the room, shared a nod. If the man at the podium had noticed Billie missing, he made no mention of it. They would consult afterwards, compare notes on this scurvy crew. But now it was time for luncheon in the lounge, ham biscuits and lemonade served by the Fessor Doctor's wife and daughter, and their servant girls, attended by his daughter's school friends in their autumn gowns. The students grinned at that, took their first easy breaths of the morning, and happily dropped their books and bundles in a corner. Those empty tables, the uppity boy in his butcher's apron, the grand atrium with the glass skylight, the preachy teacher, the nauseating smells, a lot to absorb all at once. But girls and lemonade and tea cakes, that's the doctoring dream they'd come for.

Chris watched them go, then headed down the back stairs to check that all was in order for the first day of class. Two stiffs in the cooling cave, necks stretched from the weekend's hanging on the city gallows down the hill, quite rigored, and bellies ripening, but they'd likely hold up. He and his father would pull them out in the evening under lantern light to peel their faces and arms, maybe gut them if they were too gassy already. He took his paddle to the lye vat and dug for bones in the gruel. With long tongs, he pulled out a pelvis and spine still connected, that was good. Had to poke around for the jaw and hands, finally gave up on the toe bones. These days, Chris could stand over the fuming vat without a mask, knew how to temper his breath, inhale shallowly, let the funk get him dizzy so his stomach wouldn't turn. It was one of the proofs he was ready for this work. He laid out the bones on a tarp, framing a skeleton as he went. Next month he'd throw them all together like a puzzle, so the boys would have to make up a shape, but they didn't know squat yet, so this first time he'd do it himself.

When he had tipped the vat into the pit and rinsed it out with water from the cistern, had scrubbed his hands till they stung, and hung up his leather apron, he went to the cupboard and pulled out a hard tack biscuit and an apple from a gnarled old tree at the edge of the pauper's field. He ate on his stool next to his father's rocking chair, tossing crumbs to the cats. He had one more apple. He peeled and sliced it with his scalpel, chewed the long strip of peel as he mashed the naked flesh with the flat of his hand so the old man could gum the pulp, and carried it on a saucer into their room. How odd, he thought, to find his father abed past dawn. For a moment he allowed himself a flicker of pride that he'd been trusted with the all-important introductions and with the preparations for the launch of another school year. And then a shock shot up his spine like he'd stepped on a snake, when he saw that the eyes of the old man lying flat on the pallet stared blindly at the ceiling, dry as marbles.

CHAPTER 9

PRICE'S FUNERAL HOME - JACKSON ADDITION

"I WILL NOT TAKE HIM, NO."

Alfred D. Price — who insisted on the title funeral director rather than the demeaning term undertaker that so many still used, whose Duval Street parlor sported paired stained glass windows, lilies of the valley and a winding grape vine climbing a radiant field of bluebird bright panes that seemed to ripple like water as the sun poured in, installed either side of the walnut double doors and the one step entrance amenable to pall bearers, who wore a silvery gray suit and tie that set off his shock of white hair, with a white carnation at the lapel, every day of the week — stepped from behind his desk and peered out the back window at the boys scrubbing the better hearse for the Reverend Smith's funeral on Sunday afternoon. He lifted the window and shouted to polish her good, especially the cut glass side panels that would show off the ivory-white coffin with its gold-plated handles, as the procession made its way up to the cemetery.

Reginald Scott, his chief associate, stood with derby hat in hand, eyes narrowed and lips pressed tight, considering closely what he was about to say. Director Price shut the window against the noise and the autumn chill, turning back with a look of surprise that Scott had not dismissed himself already.

"Alfred," Scott said, "This is no charity case."

"I know that. What is your point?"

"The dean of the medical school has asked for a cortege, has offered an upfront fee, a plot at Cedarwood, inside the walls."

"For a man who was his slave."

"Sir?"

"Since he was a boy, yes, locked him down in that hellish place, the college building, they say they built the Egyptian monstrosity around him."

"He has family. A son."

"Yes, his son, his errand boy. Scrofulous type, scurries about, people spit when he passes."

"Yessir, name of Chris. That's the thing, you see."

"The thing I see is this, Reginald. It is our high mission here at Price's to accord the dead all due respect, to assure the future repose of the soul and the comfort of mourners. But this man! This man, at the bidding of these doctors, has despoiled what we had hoped would be the final resting place of those entrusted to our care, ripped the deceased from their graves, bared their flesh to the knives of knaves, left them in fragments for vermin to gnaw, and in doing so has condemned their souls – their souls, do you hear? – to an eternity in limbo or worse. This man, this ghoul, known and feared by all, labored in opposition to all we strive to uphold in our sacred work. Were we to allow his corpse inside these walls? I fear we'd be burned to rubble if we were to desecrate our parlors in this way. We'd be run out of town like as not."

"Yessir, but I been with you a long time. You done business with ol' Billie. Back before the war."

"Stop now."

"It was them doctors who got you goin', five dollars a stiff, you 'member that?"

"Do not speak of that again." He pounded a fist onto the desktop, gaveling the matter closed. Scott was a good man, loyal, even dared to speak a hard truth in confidence. But good men came cheap these days.

"So what the dean say when I tell him no?"

"I will speak to the dean. We have an understanding. Half a dozen undertakers in Jackson Addition, he can choose one of them."

"It's a good chunk of money, though."

"Reginald, cease. Consider the good chunk of money required to replace our windows should a stone come in!"

"Yessir, that, too." He half bowed. "I leave it there then."

The funeral director took his seat, tossing a licorice candy to his partner. "Reginald, I grasp your thinking, but you must understand, we are just now emerging from a dark hell, you know this, to a more enlightened time when folks have come to dote on their deceased, want them sent along with ceremony. Might not have a pot to piss in, but Grandpa going out in glory. That's the business we're in now, that's where Price's Funeral Home makes its stand. We take this body, even if nobody says a word, our reputation will suffer. And you must know in this line that's all a man has. One foot placed wrong, one miscue such as this, would send us back amongst the pack again. If nothing else, the dean will understand that."

IN THE END Chris did it himself. The college agreed to the expense of a pine coffin, the flimsy kind carpenters knocked together in minutes known as toothpick boxes, but Chris dug into the pallet mattress for a handful of cash and on the way to the cemetery halted the ambulance at a blacksmith's, instructing the man to secure the box with barrel staves. Helping Chris pull the casket down out of the carriage, the blacksmith surmised who Chris was, and smirked, "Word get out the body snatcher of Richmond trust these here barrel staves to keep a stiff in the ground, we have undertakers lined up 'round the back alley 'fore long."

Further down the street at the stockyard Chris purchased two bales of hay that he squeezed alongside his father's coffin, stopped at a rooming house on Clay Street for the student who'd been volunteered to help, and turned north on Second Street towards Poor House Hill in broad daylight, passing the glittering storefronts of Jackson Addition funeral homes, all of which had refused his father's body. Stoic in the driver's seat, he ignored the people who pointedly kept their hats on as the ambulance passed, those who spat or turned their backs. The student beside him noted, "Folks know who this is in here, don't they?"

Chris gave no reply, only chucking the horse to maintain their stately pace.

No rules for where to lay a body down on the pauper's slope, but Chris knew exactly where to dig, just beyond the root span of his father's old sycamore tree. Leafless and bone white, here in the fall, the spectral trunk rose like a mighty skeleton lifting its crooked fingers to the gray sky, and the hollow at its base glowered like a mouth set in a mourning pout. Chris and the student wrestled the coffin to the ground, pulled out the hay bales, shovel and gunny sack, and Chris nodded for him to go. The student backed away embarrassed, but drove the ambulance out of the cemetery, leaving Chris and his work alone. For the first time, he stood among the dead as a mourner, peering about at the wooden stakes set in terraced rows down the hill. He could not recall all the places he and his father had dug; everything looked so different in daylight. He noticed with approval that this cemetery out at the north edge of town was just far enough from the factory racket on the river so you could make out birds chirping and high enough above Shockoe Creek so the winter rains did not upfloat the coffins, as they had downstream near the college in the day.

He took off his father's suit jacket, which fit him well, and picked up a shovel. All afternoon he labored to make a deep hole, numb to any feeling. Alone, he tipped the pine box into the grave, wrestled it flat, then stood atop it to crawl out onto the leaf-strewn lawn, at last taking a moment to think. He watched a funeral cortege coming through the walled gates to the adjoining private cemetery, paired white horses with tall, feathered topknots pulling a glass-sided carriage that led a marching band honking a dirge and a trailing line of mourners in their Sunday clothes. On a far hill, diggers stood aside before an open grave. Chris thought he recognized one of them, fellow his father had hired to help out at night on occasion. Wished he'd thought to ask him.

As the mourners gathered around the distant grave, Chris turned back to work. "The way you do it," he spoke aloud, "you throw down some dirt, get a good thick pile, then toss in a batch of hay, spread it out across the dirt. Cover that with some more dirt and criss-cross the hay again and keep goin' like that till you fill the hole. Now you try and dig that up."

It was dusk by the time he finished, the mourners across the way long gone. He mounded the dirt smooth and tamped it down with his shovel, finally pausing to make a promise to the man in the ground. "If Mama ever come, I'll bring her here." He took a seat on a blanket of fallen leaves beneath the old tree and gnawed a biscuit as night fell. Bats prowled the air, clicking. He tapped the bulge of his father's pistol in his gunny sack. He'd never fired the gun, but said aloud, "Any man come, he ain't leave this graveyard walkin'."

The work was on him now, he realized. Or not. Good time to go off, try something else. But the Fessor Doctor had paid for the toothpick casket, had loaned out the ambulance and a student volunteer. Had said nothing yet, but surely hoped Chris would stay. He considered the makeshift tent city on Mayo Island, the factory laborers limping in to work, the farm boys bent to tobacco already, as if the war had never happened. A man with a trade ought to keep it, is what the old man would say.

He thought of all the nights he'd sat out past midnight with his father under this tree, waiting for the right time to act. Sometimes Billie would whittle in the dark, carving by touch: a duck, a whistle, a pipe. Chris had a dozen of his creations lined up on a shelf in the basement room they'd no longer share. The old man always seemed so peaceful by this tree, he thought, and now he could rest on through time where he lay. People ought to have that courtesy, he mused, to rot whole down in one place.

Before the rain, a wind picked up and made the bare tree's branches rattle. Chris startled at a shadow lumbering past, like somebody hauling brush in their arms. He pulled the knapsack close. Not a drop of rain had fallen, it was still dry on the hill, when a lightning bolt split the old tree and threw Chris ten feet in the air, timber crashing as the trunk caught fire and blazed. He came awake to cascading rain, the shattered tree sizzling about him, and thunder roaring as a brutal storm threw down on the city. He couldn't move, screamed in terror into the torrent, then realized he lay pinned by a tree limb, not a bone cracked or broken, though he was soaked through and through. No question, somebody in the dark was laughing uproariously at it all, a tumble of voices caught up in the wind.

Chris dragged himself out from under the broken tree, found his boots in the muck, then crawled to his father's grave, and dropped flat upon it, wailing in fear and shock, his body muddied as his fingers clawed the earth. He was there at dawn, still quaking and half awake, when the laundry lady passed on her way to the alms house and glimpsed the scorched ruins of the old sycamore. At first she feared the man sprawled on the grave was a corpse, floated up from its grave in the downpour. When she bent to touch the man's arm, his head lifted and stunned eyes stared up from his muddied face, so she startled. Then the little man, she recounted later to her mistress, seemed to grasp his situation, the shame of it or something, got up on his hands and knees and scurried off down the hill, like an animal in men's clothing, a terrible sight.

"You seen a duppy," she was told, "devil riz up from that grave. That old Billie's spot, he just interred yestiddy. You seen his soul scurry off to hell is what. Lucky he ain't take you! Satan slapped that tree down when he come, we all heard it, haul his ass off to damnation."

But that wasn't what she'd seen at all. She'd seen the frightened face of a young man, a boy, really. And she pitied him for whatever he had been doing out there. That bereft and terrified expression. Poor orphan boy out on such a frightful night.

———

At the basement door, Chris kicked off his muddy boots, then slipped inside barefoot, locking the door behind. His gunny sack, the shovel and the pistol, all left behind at the cemetery. He'd have to go back and get them, a thought that made him quail. Then a new thing shamed him when the ugly odor of the basement came for him, first time he'd puked in years. Who was he now, what happened out there, what was this place anyway? His ears rang and his soiled coat stank of smoke. It felt like his brain had flipped upside down in his head, that maybe he, like his father, had fallen.

He felt for a candle and lit it with trembling fingers. Eyes not his own scanned the dank workshop. Everything before him quivered. In the candle's dim light, sharps glinted their ragged teeth, the open pit emitting a viney vapor that flickered hypnotically next to the lye vat foulest of all, its sour stench reaching out to grapple at his throat. It was like he'd never seen this cellar before, had never understood what went on in here, where now the spirits of all the dead had decided to come on in and crowd about, seeking out their corporeal bits, hissing and taunting the culprit at the door.

He stumbled through the workshop, waving an arm as if knocking down cobwebs in his way, a wailing sound ringing from the walls. The sound was his own, rising unbidden in his throat, a voice he'd never heard before, broken and sobbing and forlorn. He crashed into the sleeping closet, slammed the door behind him, and fell to his knees before the pallet he'd shared with his father his whole life. The quilt thrown off, the pillow still bearing the imprint of the old man's head, tobacco pipe dead and cold on the stone floor.

He crawled to the pipe and cradled it in his lap. Rocked it like a baby small as it was. Let himself wail along with the lost souls hunkering about, sang it down to a humming in time, a low moan that marked the turn, that he understood would henceforth be the foundation music for whatever else might come.

The candle had all but guttered when he finally got to his feet and set the pipe on the shelf with his whittled toys. His brain felt like it was just about flipped back where it belonged. Down here in the stone foundation not a sound but a slow dripping, like a clock's ticking, from the dungeon behind. Navigating by touch in the familiar darkness, he stripped down and drew cold cistern water for his bath, didn't bother to heat it, just sank into the tub and let the clear chill liquid wake him to the world as it was. Used the lye soap that burned his soft parts and that was a medicine, too, helped his brain settle in between his ears, that good fit on the skull pan where it belonged. Lungs pumping in his chest regular, not quite ready to face facts.

He climbed out of the tub dripping and blue, tossed his one good shirt into the water, then the muddied and charred jacket and pants. They could soak, maybe they were salvageable. All he had left were his work clothes, the greasy slacks, the gray undershirt, and the collarless wool sweater, stained past any bleaching. He found his black skull cap, padded with cotton, that had replaced his unwieldy turban, and locked the cell behind him. Late afternoon, people still about, they would scoff and look askance, but he had to go back to the cemetery. Food would help, he knew. Since puking he'd felt floaty, balloon-like, but now the hunger chewed his guts, urged him on. Maybe a windfall apple along the graveyard wall.

It hadn't been a dream, was weirder than that. He looked up at the void in the sky where the towering sycamore had stood, saw its scorched half trunk and the heavy limbs strewn on the ground. Like a human skeleton from the boiling vat, melted to bone, a scattered puzzle. But as he strode up the hill he noted, too, someone was standing at his father's grave. Had the snatcher's come anyway, storm or not? Had they shoveled through the straw, pried open the sealed lid, torn open the coffin and sacked his father's body?

A young woman all in white and a starched white apron. She nodded as he approached, tucked her chin and spoke first, "I expected you'd come."

The red mud atop the grave had settled in the storm, but seemed otherwise undisturbed.

She said, "I believe you left this, this is yours?" She lifted the soggy gunny sack and handed it across the grave to him. Who was this? When was the last time anyone had spoken kindly to him outside the college walls?

He looked about, asked, "Did you see a shovel?"

She shook her head. "This sack lay up by the blasted tree. Such a storm last night!"

He cinched the bag open and found the pistol inside.

The girl said, "Are you alright now?"

She was smiling, not meanly, but sweetly. He caught himself staring.

She said, "This is your father's grave, is it not? I wish his soul peace."

"You know that? You know me?"

"Asked about today. Saw you this morning on my way to the alms house. I help with the laundry there."

"This mornin'? Here?" What would she have seen?

"Stopped again on my way home in case you might return."

Of all the events of the past day, no doubt this was the strangest. "What you know of me?" he asked, eyes downcast to the grave between them.

"Everyone knows you, Chris Baker." She used his Christian name.

"Call me a monster."

"I found you stretched on your father's grave. No monster would do that."

"This mornin'?"

"Do you remember?"

"Buried him myself. Took a rest under the old tree."

"The thunder bolt must have stunned you. You are very fortunate, I think."

His frown eased then. Of course, this was an angel and yes he had passed to the other side. His body lay dead under the sycamore, broken and burnt to crisp. He pulled off his skullcap, bent to one knee, and whispered, "Bless you."

"Oh, get up boy. Done nothin' for all that. Take your gunny and go home now, will you?"

He forced himself to gaze up at her round gentle chin, her high proud cheekbones, those tender questioning eyes. The last woman who had spoken a kind word to him, or any word at all, really, had gone out for a Christmas chicken years ago and disappeared off the face of the earth. He could not stand. She walked around the grave and bent to take his arm. She touched him! Without malice. With a firm and unafraid grasp. Helped him to his feet. They stood side by side, the muddy grave mound before them and the sky ablaze at sunset.

"I'm late to home," she said.

He couldn't reply. He watched her turn in her white dress, glide out of the cemetery, step onto Hospital Street and dwindle down the hill. Then he dropped cross-legged beside the grave and rummaged in his sack for the pistol. His now to do with whatever.

Twilight came on, revealing a half moon, white as bone, staring cockeyed down at the city. If all this day was not a last breath dying dream; if his tears tasted salty. If that sweet angel was only what she said she was.

Funny, he thought, how you don't see it move, but how the moon hides its path in plain sight, sneaking so slow on its way.

CHAPTER 10

1869

"WHEN DID you start giving them names, Chris?" one of the students asked.

"Ain't know, just did."

He knew. It was the harrowing days after his father died, when all the burden fell on him and for that first semester seemed too much. There were things the old man hadn't taught him properly yet, and the work was too much for one man alone, so maggot-livid body parts putrefied to grease on the butcher block, bones calcified in the lye vat before he could fish them out, the basement floor thickened with blood and offal that made a sucking sound with every step. Rats overran the cats, so there were squawling fights in the dark corners night and day, and it was all he could do to get a fresh stiff in for the students when needed. He'd cowered more than one night in a cemetery ditch, while a mourner with a gun and a torch called him out. He didn't sleep, threw up anything he tried to eat, any gasp of fresh air out the back door made him swoon. Mid-term, the Fessor Doctor had to take him aside to get him to wash his grisly clothes.

But the worst of it was the incessant voices of the haints, all around him, his ears ringing with their whining accusations. He'd catch a glimpse of something turning in the rotten fumes rising from the pit or a flicker in the shadows where the cats and rats brawled. He'd feel a hot draft at his neck as if someone breathed down his collar. The pallet where his father had died bucked him off when he tried to lie down. But he had work to do, everything from raking the front steps and mopping the halls to digging up cadavers and teaching the students how to cut, and then disposing of the remains, a 24-7 proposition now that it was just him to do it all.

So that was when the naming of the stiffs first started, a halting effort to get control of the situation. On occasion, he had come across while still breathing the bodies he later unearthed. The hanged prisoners were known, so he'd make up a nickname for their corpses, like you would for a schoolboy. Ronald became Rotten Ronnie, Samuel Stinky Sam. The anonymous corpses he named based on what they looked like – Fatty, Peg Leg, Nosey – but in a week of anatomy class each one broke down to its component parts, while the students raced to dissect their decomposing tissues, until it all ended up in one jumbled pile, nameless mush and bone tossed down the pit.

It took weeks, but he gradually found his bearing, got a system going that was different from his father's, but fit his youthful constitution. He could nap two or three times for a few minutes in the old rocker, wake up to scarf a dried persimmon and a crust of bread, and stay awake the rest of the 24 hours, lanterns burning through the long night while the haints hissed and cackled. He caged up the cats in the old Fessor Doctor's cage for two nights while he lay arsenic-laced ears around the place and killed off a slew of rats, giving the cats a fighting chance. One day he dragged the old mattress out back and hung it across a picket fence. He hammered at it with a broom until the haints shut up, then brought it inside again, and for the first time since his father's death, lay peacefully upon it.

They worried him, though. Were these swirling, taunting vapors real or some kind of waking dream? Had a thread come loose in his brain pan when the thunder bolt struck? Maddening, how they buzzed at his ears, caught the corner of his eye, tickled the hair on the back of his neck, sometimes busy as a fog of hornets around his head. Had his father suffered these annoyances? Was he alone in his inkling of these rifts in what is?

The naming helped a little, but the real medicine, he found, was the stirring. Despite the fumes and the heat and the chemical burns on his hands when the soupy concoction splashed, he thought of those hours alone after class in his basement cell as the best part of the day. Moisture dripped from the low ceiling as the lye vat bubbled, the only other sounds his own chary breaths and that tuneless hum he'd been making, paced in rhythm with the paddle. This was the first task his father had taught him. In the beginning, it was the main thing he had done to help around the college, and even now it grounded his routines.

The cast iron vat sat squat in the middle of the basement. He had to squeeze around it to get by. Bucket after bucket, he'd bring water from the cistern, then dip into a sack of lye to pour just one bucket full of the jagged gray crystals into the pot. A weird thing happened then; within minutes, the water would heat, near to boiling, and a funky vapor would rise up and fill the room, almost like a grasping hand seeking what it needed. He went upstairs to the atrium cutting room and returned with buckets of flesh and guts, then a gunny holding the meaty skeletons, and dumped it all in, giving the vat its due. His stirring helped it along.

All sorts of things happened then. Nothing he could put words to. He stood at a bubbling vat of human flesh for hours, stirring and humming, while innards and skin dissolved out into the soup, vapors danced, and the clear water grew murky as tea. He poked at the bones left floating on the skim, a grinning skull bobbing to the surface, a hand chopped clean at the wrist slowly falling apart, all its bony articulations eventually separating as its ligamentous strings liquefied, and the little finger bones going their own way, always a hassle to dig out.

There was a teaching in all this that he wasn't sure he cared to learn. Or a bitter medicine for a disease he wasn't sure he had. Whatever it was it drew him and repulsed him in equal measure as he stirred. The fetor deepened with the body's melting, and each night when the work was done, when what was left in the vat was a disaggregated skeleton and the makings of soap, he went to the back door, stood there gulping the night air, and if no one passed, if no one shouted or threw a rock, then came a moment that glued him to the spot. His ponderings then were frightening, and intriguing, and worrisome, and beckoning. The vapors all up in his lungs whispered tantalizing secrets just the other side of understanding. Where, he told them, they rightly belonged.

THAT TERM CAME to an end none too soon. He used the summer to get his sea legs, so by the time cold weather arrived and it was time to dig again, he had the college building in pristine shape, smelling like apple cider vinegar when the boys rolled in for their first class, two consumption victims from the alms house prepped and ready in the basement. The Fessor Doctor strode in with his box of textbooks, nodded to the new boys, and waved an arm his way. "This is Chris Baker, our janitor and diener. You will treat him with all due respect."

The Interview

"I know that you must be a very busy man, famous among the physicians who have studied here at the Medical College. Have spoken to several of our local doctors, and each one has a favorite anecdote, it seems, about their time here under your instruction."

"Which ones you talk to? I 'member 'em all, just about."

"Well, Dr. Tompkins, your dean, tells of how recently a vendor offered a wax frame skeleton for demonstration purposes."

"Them fools do come knockin'."

"Said you took one look at his mock skeleton and noticed it was missing a row of ribs."

"That and no knee caps, neither."

"Said he hadn't made that observation himself, nor any of the students."

"Well, that's what they come here to learn. Ain't expected to know what they don't know."

"Another tale, would be interested in your side of the story, Dr. Douglas of the Medical Board, doesn't claim he was involved in this, only heard it the next day from another student, so he says. Well, this young man, after a night-time foray into a local cemetery, on return hid under a tarp in the carriage, I believe he said, lying right alongside a disinterred corpse?"

"They done that many a time."

"Hmm. And then proceeded to emit ghostly moans and calls to frighten you?"

"Did he say they scared me?"

"In this case, no, seemed you were quite comfortable with the unearthly humming and joined right along with it, made up a tune of sorts, and just drove your buggy with its ghastly freight along back here to the college."

"He tell you the next part?"

"*How you took out a saw and planned to cut off the corpse's legs while it yet lay in the wagon?*"

"*Said it be lighter to haul the pieces in. Made sure the boy heard that.*"

"*Ending his ruse right there.*"

"*He jump up like a gandy-dancer out that wagon bed.*"

"*Were you upset at his antics?*"

"*Them boys, they got a long road in this college, ain't all of 'em able to get through it. Believe the ones tried that trick on me did alright, though.*"

"*So, you are not a superstitious man?*"

"*You mean haints bother me?*"

"*Yes, that, I suppose.*"

"*My job ain't about haints, it's stiffs I'm after, and ain't one of them ever chase after me.*"

"*Well, our readers will be grateful to hear that from an expert such as yourself.*"

"*Ain't no other expert such as myself.*"

"*No, I understand, indeed, your reputation precedes you.*"

"*Yessuh. For good or no, you can put your feet on that.*"

CHAPTER 11

1870

THESE NEW STUDENTS no worse than the usual crew. Squeamish, green at the gills, mincy, but the way boys do, acting haughty about it, seeking to hide their qualms with teasing. When the Fessor Doctor was around, they aped his high style. Baker watched them each learn that patrician sniff, that somber bending to the corpse, the delicate carving with the scalpel, pinky finger held erect as if at dinner. This was the week that boggled their childish minds, always a lot to juggle, and not always a feat he could pull off, but this time the logistics had worked out. A young veteran from the infirmary upstairs handed over fresh on the promise they'd bag up his leavings and remand him for fancy burial up in the new Hollywood cemetery, all this negotiated by the Fessor Doctor, who'd come to the boy's side in his raving, but too late. Had gouged out his own eyes with a spoon, dug deeper to the gray matter in behind. The eyes salvaged, too, plump in a jar of rum on the table beside the corpse.

For this exposition, Baker had brought up a second table, upon which lay what was left of a millworker, whose leg crushed in the millstone had rotted him up as he sweated in his tent, already stinking of death. Baker had found him, paid a dollar to haul the body straight out of the tent, no burial at all, no family and y'all keep his kit. So here they lay side-by-side on the steel slabs, one with no eyes, the other with one leg, but otherwise intact. One pale-skinned, the other dark, offering a pointed lesson beyond the usual "where do all the pieces fit" puzzle.

The Fessor Doctor made no mention of this fact. Let their eyes see for themselves, if they would. Chris waited, he could time it to the minute, for the whispered, "You take the dark meat" joke. These stiffs would last the week, if they could cut the guts out this morning. He would saw them in half at the pelvis, try to preserve the three lower limbs in salt while they worked over the torso. A lot to get done in a hurry, but the usual caution carried a new overlay on this day. Where to start? Which one more of a violation than the other? Of course, they'd cut up black and white bodies before. Even a woman's already, and that baby with the swollen head. But given a choice between the races, they always hesitated. The disgust of handling the dark-skinned body versus the dishonor in violating the paler one. A lot to think about, and time's a-wasting.

The Fessor Doctor had mused to Baker once that maybe two of the ten would grasp his point, that human bodies are all essentially the same. They weighed the hearts and brains against each other, made sure to tape-measure the reproductive apparatus. Carving past the epidermal tissue, the muscle and tendon of both corpses glistened in identical purpling shades. Their stench blended in the stale air. Those two curious students would come to the Fessor Doctor later, worried and fretful, demanding that he explain what they had seen. He would play the politician, offering sherry, saying nothing, letting them sort out the conundrum for themselves. He knew, as they did not, of the anatomy professor in Baton Rouge, tarred and feathered and sent riding out of town on a mule, for pulling just such a comparison stunt. Any word he said might get back to the rabble. So he played it as coincidence and left the students to their own musings, as over the next week they reduced the paired corpses to bucketed gruel for the cats who prowled at their feet.

CHAPTER 12

1872

NO ANATOMY CLASS in the Summer; stiffs rot too fast in the heat. Fessor Doctor off to France, students doing their book learning and all the cutting they wanted on live folks upstairs at the infirmary, no more digging till Fall. Baker pulled out crates of bones he'd boiled clean in the lye bath and pieced together skeletons for the college in Charlottesville, for the museum up in Washington (the director there had additionally requested a box of skulls), and for a new client, a traveling medicine show. Patiently, over the course of several days, he chiseled pin holes in all the bones, then threaded them together with bailing wire, finally screwing a hook into the skulls and hanging the gangly things upright on a clothes line. They dangled side by side, naked of flesh, but for the first time since the dissection table discernably human. He tried to remember the person each skeleton was, man or woman, black or white, old or young, and what grave they came from. But it was hard to keep it all straight, when he'd supplied thirty bodies to the college, twenty more to the competition, just this term.

When incomplete skeletons turned up, he tried to pair the

pieces as best he could, but he had clients for the leftovers, too. Barbers bought jaws to fashion dentures with the teeth, and every scholar sought an intact polished skull for his library. They didn't deal directly with Baker, though, as no one cared to be seen at the college. He'd drop a box of bones at the back door of a pawn shop on Franklin Street on a moonless night, reach under the step for a bottle of Clear and a bag of coins, and have the bottle drunk by the time he got back to the basement, stepping stealthy as a ghost in the shadows.

He stashed the side money in his pallet, nobody need to know. Had developed a winter market, too. That's when the folk doctors came calling. They sought vials of blood, eyeballs and ears and what was left of a stillborn baby after the students carved it out. One old hoodoo gave him a ten-dollar gold piece for the special item he'd requested, destined for a shrine in the woods, what he called the world's most powerful totem, a woman's privates. He'd sold gallons of lye vat tallow to the candlemaker in the Slip. And yes, he'd used a bone saw to shave off buckets of tree bark that had tanned human hide for fancy wallets carried unbeknownst by half the legislators on Capitol Hill. Under his father's old contract, Baker earned two dollars a body from the college during school term, and that cash did add up, but he earned at least as much from his side gigs.

Saving money was key to his crazy idea. It was impossible, might as well dream of flying to the moon, but he couldn't shake it, so had decided to carve into it one slice at a time. He had a small opening in late summer when the first cut might be tried. By then with the narrow windows open all the time, the floor polished and the pit covered over, after boiling wrinkled windfall apples in the vat all day, the college building smelled almost tolerable, a vinegary aroma wafting on whatever there might be of a July breeze. That's when he dared to venture onto Broad Street to purchase new work clothes, and this year – in keeping with his fantasy – a black wool suit, linen shirt, side button dress shoes, and a derby hat.

The proprietor crossed himself a half dozen times during the transaction and spoke behind a scented napkin held close across his face, though Chris was fairly certain three baths in lye had scrubbed off the worst of the stink. It was just a habit people had around him now, though the salesman seemed to have no problem taking cash from his hand. He carried the bundle back home in a protective crouch, the new hat perched on his head. The shopping crowd on Broad Street parted for him in reproach like he was the devil himself. Back in the basement, he stripped down to a towel and burned his old clothes in a barrel out back. Then he heated another tub of water and bathed again before donning the scratchy new suit to step out on Day One of his mission.

Wednesday afternoon, at the First African Baptist Church, just around the corner but it might as well have been in India, that's where she would be, attending choir practice. He'd seen her go in, he'd seen her come out, every week without fail all through the spring term. He didn't know what he'd do, maybe just listen at a distance, so he paused by a window in the shade of the church's lee side and cocked an ear.

This was the most beautiful thing in his life, the only beautiful thing in his life, really. A heavenly aria floated on air free for the listening three days a week. Since his father's death, he'd tried to shape his days around choir practice and Sunday service, lurking by a window and lost in the soaring harmonies. Sometimes even during an anatomy lesson, while the boys fretted and teased and sawed away, rehearsal music filtered into the atrium from the nearby church, dim but gorgeous, and his eyes grew briefly misty.

The woman he had named Angel in his dreams sang in that choir. She came and went through the wide double front doors.

Sometimes alone, sometimes with other women, but never, yet, with a man. He knew that would change, he must act, but since their unimaginable conversation in the cemetery, standing at his father's grave, she had only grown more unreachable in his mind, almost be-winged and haloed, and he feared he would drop dead if she spoke to him again. But he must. Here in his new suit, smelling of patchouli and apples, fingernails paired, teeth polished, if not today, when?

The music ebbed and swelled, the men laying down a swaying beat deep as rushing water on which the women's voices dipped and sailed. The church's mighty organ hummed, testing them, egging them on, making the church walls themselves seem to quiver. The rehearsal went on and on, at first exciting, then gradually exhausting him. He slumped on a bench in the shade, derby hat on his lap, new shoes crossed at the end of his outstretched legs, and fell into a doze.

"Mr. Baker. Are you well?"

He roused, saw his hat on the ground and reached for it, wiped away spittle at his mouth.

"I didn't mean to disturb you, sir."

It was she. "Angel." He dared to speak her name.

"Angel, sir? Oh no, do you recall? I'm the laundry girl, Martha. We met that sad day for you, up the hill?"

He sat up and tried to straighten his lapel, confused and certain he was dreaming. "Oh, Martha, it is? Yes, so sorry, I was...."

"You were napping and I woke you and for that I apologize."

"No, please, I...."

"May I sit, sir?"

"Oh yes, do." He scooted to one end of the bench and nodded towards the empty seat.

"You came for the singing?"

"Oh, that yes, I enjoy the choir. You sing in there, too?"

"I do. Soprano row. Since I was little."

"You sound like heaven, all of you."

"Yes, well, sometimes I think so, too. Bless you, sir."

"Miss Martha, I wish to thank you for your kindness that day." These were the very words he had rehearsed for weeks, had imagined himself speaking on a knee in a garden among twittering songbirds.

"Mr. Baker, my heart ached for your pain that day."

"My daddy."

"Yes, your only kin, am I correct in that? You are alone."

"Yes."

She paused then, allowed her eyes to gaze up at the tall church window, then turned her head down the street to the weird old college building. At last she asked, "Do you ever come to church?"

"Oh no. Like to sit here and listen."

"You come here during service?"

"When I can get away." He couldn't move; dared not meet her gaze for fear she'd up and flit away.

"The church can be a family, too, Mr. Baker."

"Miss Martha, you surely must know what I do."

"We all must do something, sir."

"But the congregation, they would not...."

"No man should be alone entirely," she said.

"No, ma'am, reckon not."

"Will you come again?"

"You mean here?" At last he braved a look at her gentle face, haloed by a prim straw hat.

"Yes, Mr. Baker, here. I will look for you Friday, and may bring you a butter biscuit, too."

She smiled, angelically, and stood. All in white, even her crocheted shawl. He tried to stand, to bow, to kneel, to somehow acknowledge this anointment, but he could not rise. He nodded,

"Yes, ma'am," stupidly, and watched her walk out of the church shadow back onto Broad Street again. His hands shook; he felt faint. And was almost grateful for the rock that struck just behind his ear, breaking the spell, and sending him scurrying back to the basement in a fret.

CHAPTER 13

1874

BOYS WERE WAITING when he came up on the lift with the cadaver, pretending to be all casual and uninterested, but as the body rose to the occasion, they always cut a look his way, to see what come out the ground this time. The lift halted with a shudder. Baker reached across the corpse's midsection so she wouldn't slide, then shoved the wheeled table out under the skylight. When he pulled the sheet away, the boys gasped, as he'd expected, this one a young woman, well situated, though her flesh had gone purple as a bruise, and her face belied her body's repose, the mouth wide in rictus, eyes squeezed shut, as if aware of the horror to come. The obnoxious death vapor rose from her lips, but she was pretty fresh, her joints just beginning to loosen. One of them stiffs looked like they might sit up and give a boy a slap.

"Fessor Doctor here? Demonstrator?" he asked, though he knew the answer already.

"Opera last night," one of the students smirked.

"Then the gambling tables," said another. No one stood, all slouched along the benches puffing cigars, no doubt hoping this class, too, would be canceled.

"Hey Chris, you see the paper this morning? Look here." One student unfolded the newspaper and held it up for display with both hands. "You made the front page again."

"Called this place Chris Baker's College!"

Baker frowned. "Put that mess away, son. They just stirrin' the pot."

"No, wait now, my dear sir." The student stepped to the professor's podium, newspaper unfurling in his hands. "Allow me, as it seems you are the true captain of this institute, its engine and its driver, too, I think all will agree."

"Come down off there, Slusher. We got cuttin' to do. Ain't want to hear all that."

The student paused for effect, the others taking their places in the atrium seats, Baker standing impatient alongside the cadaver.

"Front page, Times Dispatch, this morning, reads thusly: A Study in Real Life: Chris Baker and His 'Subjects' – that word in quotes! – An Outcast to His People! – Cheerful Among Corpses! And this last line of the heading, are you ready, gentlemen? – A Queer Darkey!"

Baker shook his head, "Queer darkey, they say? Got that part right. Come here now, boys, she ain't hold up firm like this forever. Y'all help me get her up on the cuttin' board. Fessor Doctor or no, y'all need to get this skull opened up you want to graduate."

"But Chris, the article goes on to say you do black magic, voodoo, got your own trunk line to the devil himself!"

"You see some black magic with the back of my hand you don't come off that stage mighty quick."

"Alright, Doctor Queer Darkey," he laughed.

One by one, reluctantly, the students ground out their cigars and donned rubber aprons, grimacing as they gathered to lift the surprisingly heavy corpse onto the metal table. This was always the hardest part of dissection, the first touch, engagement with the dead. The rest, they had learned, was a gradual strangling of the initial revulsion, each day's dissection a little less daunting.

"Gentlemen, one of you boys done read your book. We gon' take her skull off, get her brain out 'fore it turn to mush. Where do we start? You, Cunningham, what you say?"

The student called on pulled a handkerchief from his shirt pocket, wiped his glasses briefly, then lurched for a bucket on the floor, where he discharged his breakfast.

"Starke, you read the chapter? Get your scalpel, here, what we do first?"

The sallow-faced youngster edged towards the head of the table, scalpel in hand, and bent to the face locked in its ghastly expression. "Might we cover up the rest of her, while we work on her head?" he asked.

"You want to, sure." Starke and another student retrieved the oil cloth tarp and covered the corpse from the neck down, tucking in the corners beneath the nude body as gently as they could. But her head, exposed, was the real horror, that gaping mouth, the swollen black tongue, the sickening fumes rising from the woman's rotting lungs. But there was nothing for it. Starke picked up his scalpel and gamely bent to his task.

"Well now, Chris. Shall we shave her head?"

"Hair come off with the scalp. No time for all that. Go ahead, now what you cut first?"

The other students leaned in, less squeamish now that the girl's body was covered. A shaft of sun beamed down from the skylight and lit the space as if on cue.

Baker repeated, "First cut?"

Starke answered, "Midline incision, isn't it?"

"That's right, I lift her head for you. Cut straight as you can, from between her eyes right over the top to the back of her skull. Wait now. You ever try to peel a fresh tomato? That's how finicky you got to be on this, if we gon' see all we need to here. Skin on her head shallow as that tomato, and the cap inside there is thick. You go too deep all them nerves and blood vessels get cut, too. Think tomato now, see how she peel up clean?"

The student bent to his work, lips pursed, everyone steeling themselves for their turn at the grisly procedure. Baker nodded, "That's right, now you did good. What you do now is, come right over the top again, from one ear to the other, make a x, just as slick as you was."

Clearly, the student was having difficulty with this effort. Though the room was cool, sweat dripped on the corpse's face, and his hand shook as he forced himself to go on. The trick, Baker knew, was to keep him working, focused on the task, not the subject herself.

"Now, here you go, one more good slice and we pull her back. This time, start at the ear on your side, come right across over the eyebrows, that's right, all the way to the ear on this side. Now we got her, ready to peel?"

Starke collected his forceps and tugged at the scalp, snipping connective tissue as he teased the flaps away, hair and all, and dropped them in the bucket.

Baker nodded, "Good work, young man. We make a surgeon outta you yet. Alright, now, boys, before we saw into the skull, anybody name these little wiggles here on the slope?" With his scalpel, he pointed to a fine web of veins stretching up from the woman's ear.

Cooper, the tallest member of this class, gangly and shy, stood aloof at the corpse's feet, but answered from memory as if reading from the text: "Those blue fingers are all branches of the carotid artery, rising from the throat. The white threads, those are branches of the trigeminal nerve."

"Which do what?" Baker asked.

"Pain and pleasure from the face," Cooper replied, transfixed by the look of agony on the face of the dead woman.

"Alright, Cooper, bingo. Now come on up here and saw me out the brain, will you?"

The tall student seemed to wobble side to side, like a tree in a wind, before collapsing in a heap on the floor.

"Get that ammonia bottle, will you, Jatt, see if he wake up? Meneur, you got your wits about you? Take this saw, now, day is gettin' on."

The French student, a butcher's son with hands like paws, first worked again over the criss-cross pattern traced by Cooper, displaying the epicraneous muscle that lay like a tendinous sheet across the top of the skull, then reflecting the scalp's underlayer so he could take a saw to the bone.

Baker said, "Think like you makin' a bowl, saw the skull all the way around at the hat line, and she come off clean."

Though Baker cupped the woman's head in his hands, it trembled with each pass of the bone saw, causing a trickle of bile to drip from her lips. Meneur persisted, though he appeared ready at any moment to burst into tears. At last his circumnavigation of the woman's skull was complete. Baker counseled, "You pull it off now, like takin' the lid off a box."

As the skull cap pulled away, they all paused a moment at a remarkable sight. Before them sagged a bag of wrinkled tissue, a cauliflower left in the field too long. All this young woman had ever sensed or known or imagined had once danced in that putrid gray mass, encased in a veinous sheath. Baker pointed around the table, quizzing each student on the midline and cavernous sinuses and their continuations. He slit the rubbery dura mater and stood back a moment to let rank smelling cerebrospinal fluid drip into the table troughs. This next part the students could never get right. Their hands trembled, their eyes grew misty with the noxious gases rising from the corpse, and they always rushed the most delicate steps of the procedure.

"Here," he said, "You tell me what I'm showin', I'll cut."

It took the rest of the morning to dissect the skull's contents. Baker tugged the brain out of the cranial vault and cupped its gooey mass in one hand, while snipping away its vascular connections, gnawing away with scissors to sever the spinal cord. He had them identify all of the major vessels and quizzed them on which brought blood up to the brain and which sent it back to the heart. They teased at fragile cranial nerves threaded up through the skull's base. They set the pudding-like brain on a butcher block and neatly sliced it in half down the crease across its top, then sketched its bisected sections as best they could.

As the hours passed, the necessary change gradually came upon them, the students – even the newly awakened Cooper – finding themselves absorbed in the procedure, divorced from the horror of what they were about, focused on classifying and identifying, even for long moments neglecting the viscous oil and rancid gases bubbling forth from the corpse's gaping mouth.

When they were done, Baker simply nodded, calling an end to the day's dissection lab, and tossed the torn brain into the slop bucket.

Pulling off his apron, Swisher noted, "Photographer coming next week, fellows. Chris, will you stand with us for our portrait?"

"Kind of y'all," Baker nodded. "But tell him make it quick, we got cuttin' to do here. Tomorrow mornin' we take down the thoracic cage, a lot of sawin' in that, so work for all of you. Study up. Fessor Doctor or no, we gon' break this stiff down 'fore she rots. Now y'all get on home, they's snow in the air."

"We're going to stay, Chris," Starke replied. "There's a hanging today at the jail, and the view from the rooftop here is top notch. Care to join us up there?"

"Naw, we see that poor man soon enough."

"What do you mean, Chris?" Meneur asked, relighting his stubby cigar.

"You boys know where that man end up, don't you?"

"Pauper's field, like as not," Cooper guessed.

"Who wanna come with me, dig 'im up tonight?" Baker asked.

"You will bring the hanged man here?"

"Man be gone, just the stiff left. Dig him up fresh for y'all."

Embarrassed looks passed around the room. In an hour or two they'd be staring down at the festivities in the jail yard, the centerpiece wooden scaffold, the crowd gathered to watch, and some unfortunate individual, judged guilty of a capital crime, falling to the end of a rope, where his bound body would jerk and convulse for long minutes. In a day or two, that body would end up here, on this dissection table. Material for their edification. For Baker, though, it seemed just another day on the job. What would it take, they wondered, to acquire some measure of his morbid composure? And then, too much to consider: Is that, after all, what modern doctoring required?

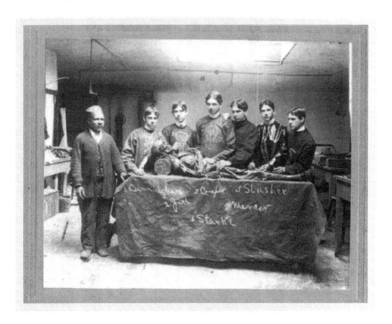

*Anatomy Lab, Medical College of Virginia,
Chris Baker on left*

The Interview

"In speaking with Dr. Matthews, I learned that, well, he so mentioned overhearing you from time to time speak to the cadavers?"

"Said that, did he? Guess I do, yeah, say a word here and about."

"What do you say to them?"

"Oh, no more'n a carpenter talk to his tools. You know, don't you splinter on me when I plane you, like that."

"For example?"

"Same thing. Don't you rot on me 'fore we get you sliced."

"Oh, I see. Your materials. Forgive me, but do you ever expect a reply?"

"'Expect or not, it come."

"The bodies speak to you?"

"They groan, they moan, they whistle. Hiss like a snake."

"They speak?"

"When the gas come on 'em, up through the throat. Fart, too, pretty loud, out the other end."

"Does that shock you?"

"Just the gas talkin' is all."

"My Lord, man, does anything frighten you?"

"Well, this one time, old lady sit right up on the table, 'bout knocked me down."

"She came back to life?"

"She dead alright. Sit up like that when the rigor hit her."

"Oh my."

"That one I did change my drawers."

"Ha. Well, I'd imagine!"

"And there is one that linger with me."

"Indeed?"

"Soldier boy, back when I was little. Daddy pulled the boy out, his fingers was bloody, nails tore off. Casket wood scratched and clawed up."

"What was it?"

"Said they put him in the ground too early, woke up in the grave."

"How horrible! Did he survive?"

"Gone by the time we got him. Daddy said he seen it like that before."

"I can see how that might, as you say, linger?"

Baker raised his head to the skylight, gazing for a long moment at a passing cloud.

"Yes," he said. "It do."

CHAPTER 14

1876

AS THEY CROSSED THE TRACKS, he took her gloved hand to help her down a stone path, to a bench he knew between broken bridges. It was Sunday and the factories quiet, the canal still. Just a gawky heron pecking near the riverbank.

"That's the unfortunate thing, Mr. Baker. Skin and bones, that's all you think we are."

She wore her yellow church dress with daisies, and looked fine in it, too. He stared out across the rippling water at bridge pylons ending midstream.

"You talkin' 'bout spirits now."

"I am." She took his elbow, so he turned to look into her gentle face. "The world isn't just what you see, sir. It's what you feel, too, and it's what you have to trust is there, even if you can't see it."

This was the true preaching; he'd heard the same from his mother in the day. How a woman can hold such a notion and it's so pretty in her face, lights up her walk, makes you want to follow. But this was not a topic he cared to pursue.

He said, "How come you with me? You know what I do."

"We do what we must is how I see it. You raised up in that business and good at it, too."

"People throw rocks, spit they see me comin'."

"People just people is all."

"Cain't bear that happen to you."

She took his hand, twining her fingers in his. "You make a good wage, and you won't always be where you at now. A lot of opportunity for a enterprising man like you."

"Enterprising man?"

"I see, I got eyes, don't I?" Eyes like melting chocolate is what she had.

"You cain't come in there, won't have that. Want you have your own house and live respectable."

"My laundry work, can run it out back of the place."

"People will talk, your business suffer."

"Got work with the hospital. Got the alms house. They're good with it all."

"Funny, I got them same contracts, too."

"See, it's what I said. Don't you worry about people."

"To me you a Angel. You know that?"

She shook her head and smiled, "I'm a laundry girl, Chris. And what these eyes have seen in my years, you're just a thing among 'em. You're a good man, a workin' man, we'll be alright."

"Can you get the stink out my clothes?

"Take a box of bleach, but yeah. You leave 'em out back, I have a change folded up for you on the porch any time."

"Tub a bath water, too?"

"With honeysuckle soap, if you can stand it," she grinned.

They sat with that notion as the river assumed the sunset's watercolor shimmer. Greens steaming in the kitchen, the little man scrubbing in the tub, maybe a child come along soap up his back. The music of her singing at her own piano. She a church girl, baking cakes for the poor, and he the city's most outcast villain, sunlight shock him dead. Who was this dear woman, he marveled, who would take up with such a man?

CHAPTER 15

1877

IT WAS NEVER GOING to be easy, of course. People talk. The scolding Martha endured from her aunties was especially choice, because sugared with understanding, speaking only to the difficulties if she persisted. You can't be seen with that ghoul. You can't bring him here to this house. People find out you're consorting with him, you'll be a target, too. He can't be right in the head to do that kind of work. Why can't he find something wholesome to do? Deacon say he got a rubber hammer, pop a boy upside the head, drag him off to his dungeon. What your mama say, she still here? When I go, praise the Lord, who say he won't tear my old bones up out the ground, chop me up like a side of beef? You hear me, girl? What you see in that man? Good men in this town working decent jobs. Your friend Maggie got herself a bricklayer. You had to work hard to find such a lowdown scoundrel. Turn over a lot of rocks. What now, you think your attentions will save his burdened soul? He just a man version of that old flea-bit mongrel you brought home in the day. Is that it? Can't see it, you going down this path. People talk; they be after you, too. Why, child, why?

To which she had no answer. It was like everything else; to

understand it, you had to be there. That morning in the cemetery after the storm, if you'd seen his eyes. Alright, yes, right then it was that same starving look the pup had. What got me started, alright. But, Auntie, that was just a minute; it's what's grown up from that. I can't tell you I'll stop. I can't tell you I know all he may be about, either. I do see the road ahead if we go down that way. My ears not stuffed with cotton. And yet, I can't tell you I'll stop, and please y'all let me be.

But they couldn't do that. Had to share every tidbit of gossip. In the laundry rooms, they made sure she heard it all. Somebody awoke to the clopping of that black horse pulling the college ambulance far after midnight. Or a mob caught him out and chased him through the graveyard, old man Cosby from our church left half out the ground. Sister nurse tell how he climb up from his smelly old basement to the infirmary upstairs, sniff around like a hang dog buzzard, waiting for a patient to pass. Somebody wing a bedpan off his head, too, send him scurrying. Fourteen graves in the old Black cemetery defiled in one week, maybe it wasn't all just him, but who else it was?

The laundry women could go at it all through the washing and rinsing and the line hanging, too, moving on from gossiping to theorizing, and always sure she got an earful. That spooky old Egyptian building is Satan's doings, and he the hand in it all. Ain't enough that a man ain't free to stand up straight in this so-called freedman's world, no rest for the weary while we breathe, but thanks to that snatcher, no rest in the grave either, and the police in the pocket of them professor doctors, look the other way. Somebody gonna get that fool. People got guns now. Man say he a cannibal, too. Eat a dead man's liver like it's pork. Anybody'd touch their lips to the lips of such a creature! Make me taste what I ate last night!

Even Reverend Holmes in her home church unloaded. Martha noted how he turned in the pulpit and cut his eye towards where she sat in the choir loft while launching into a new sermon about what awaited the congregation in the after-life. How the Salvation will reunite body and soul and we all rise together in a joyful song of praise. That is, if we still have a body. That is, if we're all in one piece. If it goes the other way, how the angels gonna find your parts, sew you back together, mighty as they may be? Where's a soul to go if the box and body he lay in is torn asunder? Seemed like a thousand pairs of eyes in all the encircling pews zeroed in on her at that moment. Some glinting with a prissy righteousness, some wet with a pitying tear, some squinting in bewilderment, but all of them judging her, this kind young woman with the songbird voice raised up in this church, baptized in our font, a home girl from out our bosom, what's gone wrong in her head?

Yet behind all of that, it only took one, one good friend to set her right. Maggie Walker, just a youngster but wise beyond her years. She said be strong. She said listen to your heart. That's where your freedom lies, that's where you hold your counsel. For all these folks, it's just something to talk about, keep them off their own worries. Maggie just a schoolgirl, straggling in late to help fold sheets, but she had big plans to teach in that same school, might even set up a night class for any laundress who cared about learning to read. She had places to go, no time for trash talk, and will you please get out my way. Alright, then, Martha told her. Bless you, Miss Maggie. Ima see what this is.

CHAPTER 16

1878

"WELL HERE HE COMES NOW, OL' St. Christopher – patron saint of lost souls, indeed!"

Mid-term was the crunch time in herding these school boys. Thought they knew it all already, having broken down a few corpses, plowed around their insides, passed their first anatomy practical. Here was when they took over the place, using the carving plinth as a poker table. Sometimes they'd lift off a fresh body, set it up in a corner, this time had even dug out his father's pipe and squeezed it between the stiff's tooth-clenched lips, before they went back to their dealing and betting. They had work to do this afternoon, tear down the lower limbs, but one said, 'Hell an arm and a leg ain't much but the same, we'll get to it in time. Tell you what, Chris, you give a sign when the Professor comes and there's a quarter in it for you."

Baker spied the bottle, half empty already in the middle of the afternoon. Hair raised on the back of his neck when he saw what they'd done with his father's pipe, but he left it there, pretended he hadn't seen, and went to stoke the stove fire, these jokers and their schemes.

He turned to see one of the farmhand boys, looked like a fox, eyes a little too close together in his face, at the gurney examining the body parts left from the previous day's dissection. He took the swollen hand of an arm lopped off at the shoulder joint and swung it in the air like a cudgel.

"Get away from there now," Baker said. "Don't be playin' with these stiffs."

He yanked the purple limb from the student's grip and pointed it at the three boys, one by one. "You ain't never seen a haint, yet, but you will. You stay 'round here, you surely will. You seen the demonstrator doctor, you seen his hand shake on the scalpel. The change come on him when the haints arrived. You be on your best behavior til then."

"Haints, my ass," the farm boy scoffed. "Chris, you just a superstitious old coon."

Baker replaced the amputated arm on the gurney, then wiped his hands on his greasy apron and shook his head. "You ain't no doctor, boy. You just a cracker field hand is all. You best pray the haints leave you be, but I ain't bettin' on you."

The other students tucked their heads, hiding grins. "Best ease up there, Chris," one chuckled.

"You knuckleheads mind what I say. You messin' with stuff you ain't know in here. I seen a boy go from hale and hearty to green and death's door in two days, he mess around in this place."

"That weren't no haints, Chris. He got the rot from a scratch."

"And how that come about? Y'all get on now till the Fessor Doctor come. I got arrangements to make for you boys." He turned to the corpse propped against the wall and yanked his father's pipe from its jaws.

And then it happened. The farm boy growled, "No n___ speak to me that way." He grabbed a bone saw off the table and slammed it down on the severed arm, imbedding it at the wrist, then jerked it away. The severed arm fell to the floor as the student grabbed Baker by the shirt front and pressed the bloody saw to his throat.

"Searcy! Put that saw down!"

It was Professor Cullen himself, arrived early to class and in the nick of time, too. Man had seen it all in the war years, and brooked no mischief since.

Baker stood firm in the grip of the angry young man, blank eyes staring sternly into his.

"Put down that saw," the professor demanded.

"N____ cussed me," the student said.

"Put down the saw. Quite enough of your shenanigans, Searcy."

"Boys, tell him what this fool called me!"

No one spoke. A cat crept over to the fallen arm and began to lick at its socket.

"Pack your belongings. You are finished here," the professor commanded.

"This is upside down, doctor, you protectin' this darkey!" the boy shouted. But he lowered the saw and gazed around at his classmates, as if really seeing them for the first time.

Baker eased the cat away with his toe, then bent to retrieve the amputated arm and place it back on the dissection table. As he knelt, a fat gob of the student's phlegm spattered on his head.

"The saw now," the professor said, holding out his hand. "We have seen quite enough, Searcy. Now go."

Chastened and confused, the student dropped the saw and reluctantly backed away. No one else moved, held in place as if posed for a camera. "We ain't done here, Chris Baker. I will get you, boy!" Searcy yelled from the stairs.

Waving a hand dismissively, the professor commanded, "Be gone!"

CHAPTER 17

1879

TWO ROOMS above a stable out past Navy Hill on the north edge of town, the loft window opening on a fenced pasture, where an old horse grazed beside a rusty Devon cow and calf, and a scrabbling gaggle of domestic geese. The clamorous, belching city sprawled out the front door all the way down to the riverfront and beyond, but Baker's first move in these quarters was to shove their board-sawn table to that window, where they might share a meal with their backs to it all.

Old Doctor Mabry had lost a leg in the war, worked out of his parlor now, but he had remembered Baker fondly, and just a word from the Fessor Doctor had won them these rooms, a trysting place away from prying eyes. No money exchanged. Rent would be laundry and mucking the stalls, which Baker reckoned was fair.

He'd bathed already in the college basement, but didn't trust his nose. Had hauled in a galvanized washtub and a pair of buckets. She'd be along, and that was the thrill of it, that she might arrive amidst his ablutions. So he didn't hurry, set the wood stove burning, climbed the stairs with water from the hand pump at the horse trough, waited with his pipe for the water to warm, then mixed in a last haul of cold water and squatted there cross-legged, scrubbing down with a lavender soap made of milder fat than lye.

Her contribution to their home awaited on the tick-straw bed up front, in a room without a window or heat source beyond the patchwork quilts she and her grudging aunties had sewn across the whole winter just for this day. She had spread them not for warmth on this gay morning of late spring, but for display, and to soften the lumpy straw mattress. Atop them lay the button-down shirt and wool slacks he'd requested. He'd given her cash and asked her to shop for them, hadn't wanted to spoil them with his gamey touch. He would pull them on only when he was sure that his skin, his hair, his nails, and his breath were free of the funk of his work.

He sat naked at the table, paring at his toenails with a scalpel, when he heard the stairs creak. He leapt up, but before he could even cover himself with a towel, she had emerged head first, her hair in long braids, her dress a white muslin like she'd worn that first day at the cemetery, and her arms embracing flowers and a basket of ripe fruit. Startled at the sight of him, she almost stumbled back down the steps, but he bent to her, pulled her up, and they fell to their first time in laughter.

HOURS LATER, he sat dumbstruck in his new clothes at the table, unable to nibble from the bowl of cherries she'd set between them. She was talking, a little giddy, but about practical things, as she pulled out her braids and let her hair go wild, the late day sun aslant on her glistening cheeks. When he had held her rounded shoulders, her eager hands had gripped his back. Her lips had sought his and opened like a fluttering bird. All of her pliant and warm and wiggly, all about him, and the rush of it something like the river's rapids, so he had swum with her, spun in the eddies. Even as the crest receded, though, the waters roared in his ears.

She said, "There's this girl, name of Maggie, she's at the new Lancaster school down the hill from your college."

He said, "Look at that calf suck her mama out there."

"Her mother runs laundry with me, and Maggie used to help, but she's got a head on her shoulders, has some big plans, and says she will teach all us washer girls to read."

"How them fat geese get along on them scrawny legs?" he mused.

She stood then, set down her comb and came around the table to rest her hands on his shoulders and peer with him out the window. She said, "We'll be alright here, Chris."

"No," he replied, "This just a wayside for us. We get you a house a your own."

"Will you stay here, make this your home until we do?" Her strong, laundry-wrung fingers worked his shoulders, so his eyes closed back in the swim.

"Got to be slick with my comin's and goin's. Cain't be out in the day, you know that."

"Come in the night then. I work all day, too, you know."

He had already plotted out his route, down the slope of Shockoe Hill behind the college, and back up the gorge along the train tracks, then a climb through the pauper's graveyard that he knew best in its night shadows anyway.

"Nights I don't work, you know I be here."

"Even just an hour, if you can get away." Her lips grazed the top of his head where it was beginning to go bald.

"Will you do that? My husband."

That word.

And that fearsome gift, the dazzling press of her living flesh.

CHAPTER 18

1880

"THE TIME HAS COME to discuss salary, Chris. Will you meet me at my office suite tomorrow?"

Baker nodded, thinking of how often he'd mopped the floors of the Fessor Doctor's office, yet he could not recall ever having been invited there. For this unprecedented occasion, he thought to don the dress suit he'd bought to court Martha, now put away in a trunk in the barn loft. He'd been away for two weeks at the end of a busy semester, catching naps in the college building's basement. Every year more students, it seemed, up to fifty now, but the night-and-day work had paid off. The bandanna in his hat held a stash of dollar bills. Martha would sew them into the pillow that held their savings intended for a real house, where the baby in her belly could play.

The night sky was already taking on that familiar bruised look before dawn, when he crept into the barn and up the stairs to the loft. But he'd missed her, already off to her laundry rounds, their rooms dark and the stove cold. He emptied the bandanna into a wash bucket and covered it with a dinner plate left on her chair, then hurried to put on his suit and sneak back out onto the street. With dawn, the early risers were about, so he took the cemetery route in his work boots, carrying his good shoes in his hands, to protect them from the muck of the gorge. He made it back to the college building without incident, a little out of breath, and took a seat in the empty auditorium away from the worst of the basement's odors, awaiting the time for his appointment upstairs.

Barn loft or no, this queer old building was Baker's real homeplace. And it ran more like a living thing than a structure, the way a human body does, or any animal really. As he saw it, the low-ceilinged basement, his chief domain, represented the bowels, where nourishing decomposition took place; the infirmary floor where sick people lay moaning gasped and pumped like the structure's lungs; while up top, the three classrooms and the dissection lab made up the brain. The office suite, with its plush chairs and oaken desks, might be the strange old building's fatty liver, and the auditorium, where he sat now among rows of empty chairs, was the arms of the institution, reaching out to the people at graduation and the like. Which made all the doctors and students and patients and nurses and the cadavers, too, for that matter, the building's life blood, circulating here and there. They all came and went, but Baker knew he was the one constant, the true backbone of the place.

Hard to say, though, if the doctors agreed. The new anatomist, a Dr. Tompkins, was a graduate of the school and had stayed on working as the anatomy demonstrator, leading dissections side by side with Baker since his student days. Baker had his number, of course, how he walked a fine line between the mess buckets of dissection and the perfumed doilies of society. Perched on his throne with a *Horner's Anatomy* on his lap, while the new Demonstrator Doctor sawed away at a ribcage and the gathered students flinched at the spatter. He knew where the bodies came from. Baker climbed the stairs to the professor's suite recalling how his father had managed this conversation, hoping to follow his stoic example.

"Well, Christopher, rare to see you in these rooms!" beamed Professor Tompkins, as he stood and beckoned Baker inside the door. "Come in, will you? I hear from Dr. Watkins that your woman is in a motherly way?"

"Martha. Baby comin', yessuh."

"May we hope for a boy to carry on the dynasty here that your father inaugurated?"

"Might be nice, yessuh."

"Sit then, Chris, have a chair," offered the professor, as he re-seated himself behind the desk. The man made a study in gray; gray suit, gray hair, gray eyes, and a neatly combed gray mustache.

"Stand just fine, suh."

"Suit yourself. I will not digress." He took off his glasses and began to clean them with a handkerchief as he spoke. "My aim as anatomy professor is to reward your long service, Chris, your unique contributions to our college. As our janitor and anatomy assistant, you have maintained, one might say elevated, the good work dear Billie carried on hereabouts. No mark on your father, to say that, of course."

"No suh."

"I invited you up here this morning to set in seal, so to speak, a new arrangement that I trust you will find amenable. The college is prepared to improve your patronage to nine dollars a month, paid first Friday, a significant increase of four dollars from our current arrangement."

"Mighty kind of y'all."

"In light of the manifold services you provide and the difficulties our program has suffered since the war." He lifted the glasses to his mouth and puffed a mist onto them, resuming his rubbing with the cloth.

"Yessuh, mighty kind."

The professor reseated the glasses on his prominent nose and lifted his grey eyes. "So, Chris, you must know that our faculty have some awareness of your extracurricular efforts in the procurement of specimens for other colleges."

"Do a little of that work, yessuh."

"To come to my point, we admire and applaud your industry in this matter. By all means continue. That said, I must adjure you to commit a portion of the earnings from that effort, which, of course, engages our resources and equipment here at the college, and occupies no small increment of your own time, to support our endeavors in training the next generation of medical men for the good health of Virginians, a mission that I know you too care about immensely."

"Suh?"

"My boy, your circumspection and diligence in all you do is appreciated, is absolutely essential to maintaining our good name, not just here in Richmond, but across the South and indeed beyond the Mason Dixon line as well."

"Do what I can, suh."

"I must say we agree, and we are aware that you have developed quite an enterprise in procuring specimens for our students, but also for a network of anatomists beyond our borders."

"You get the best, always, suh, whatever you need, I can always get it."

"I do not doubt that, Chris. We are not asking you to stop serving our external clients, indeed would see you expand your efforts, and to continue our longstanding agreements at the college in Charlottesville and beyond. What I offer here today, in addition to this handsome increase in your patronage, one that I trust will find approval in your growing household, is a partnership, if you will."

"Suh?"

"Well, Chris, it appears you have attended to your acquisitional duties so well that you may have at last won a reprieve. No doubt you have heard about the legislative debate down the hill this past year, seeking to provide for our anatomical needs through means other than criminal grave robbing?"

"Boys said somethin' along that line, yessuh."

"Well, Chris, allow me to share with you news that will brighten your day immensely. We expect that in the next legislative term or two, our representatives shall have resolved the troubling contradiction that medical schooling requires cadavers for dissection yet the acquisition of this material in our usual way marks a felony liable to ten years in prison. The bill as it stands quite ingenuously would provide, at the discretion of our Medical Board, any unclaimed body from our prisons and alms houses. This material would no longer suffer burial, but delivery directly to our door, that agreement enforced by law. My good man, your grave haunting days may soon be over!"

Baker turned the hat in his hand.

"Is this not remarkable news, Chris? They aim to make an honest man of you!"

"Not a bad notion a'tall."

"But you seem unmoved. I had thought this news to your liking?"

"Can I say, suh?"

"Of course, Chris, what is it?"

"Y'all got more boys in this college every year, keepin' 'em longer, too. Been bringin' in stiffs from the poor house and jail all along."

"Chris, please, you do not need to confide your procurement activities to me."

"No suh, but that ain't enough, is all. Law or not, to keep up, we still gotta dig."

"Yes, well, I suspected as much. And I do appreciate your candor."

"You want me stop that work? Is that it?"

The professor leaned forward, spreading his pale hands flat on the desk as if to stand. "A moment, Chris. We members of the Medical Board, yes, we have discussed this conundrum. The community insists that we leave the cemeteries, the proposed legislation would provide a solution, yet as you say, the need may be greater than that law will provide."

"Believe so."

"So, this is the solution we offer. Henceforth, I shall manage correspondence with the anatomists of other colleges, and I assure you can secure additional contracts. You will share in our dealings, provided with the funds needed to procure, package and ship, and you will be granted one quarter of the profit from each specimen, which I shall tally and dispense to you monthly."

"Well, suh...."

"Let us see whether the new law provides the cadavers needed for this venture. If not, then my hope is that it will at least lessen your nocturnal efforts. I have on my desk signed contracts from Columbia College, New York, and two medical schools in Pennsylvania, requisitioning four cadavers barreled and in good repair each month of the fall and spring school terms. These in addition to your current arrangements, which shall now fall under my purview."

"Suh."

"We shall, of course, trust your ongoing diligence and delicacy in managing all elements of this project. As you are already expert in acquisition, preservation and shipping, I expect the slight additional burden, as supported by the new law and lightened by our financial arrangement, will be to your liking. Now, one more thing, you must trust me to hold to our agreement."

"Suh."

"And apart from your spouse, as one can hardly ask you to withhold such a happy turn of events from her, you will under no circumstance speak of or admit to our arrangement. Please acknowledge that you understand this point."

Baker allowed a slight nod.

"You are a useful man, Chris, key to our success and reputation. Stay well. You may rest your shovel for the summer, no need for cadavers til Fall, am I right?"

"Yessuh, cleanin' time now."

"Indeed, well, go about your business then. I shall inform the Board."

So this is the freedman's world, Baker mused, as he descended the stairs to the basement. Boss man see what Angel call a entrepreneur and want him a taste of that coin. What the man said was, new law or not, you keep diggin', boy. Haul up stiffs in quantity for all them other schools, and after the college take its cut, Martha be lucky to fill that pillow. Still, one way or another, we will get that house. Be a lotta empty graves out Oakwood way. Lord pray this old back and my shovel hold up from it all.

The Interview

"Your reputation, Chris, appears to have made its way to the colored communities even across the river to Manchester, did you know that?"

Baker scratched his nose with the stem of his pipe. "What reputation is that?"

"It's why I'm here, after all. Rumors run rife about your work. I'd like to know what the truth of it is."

"Run rife, you say?"

"The chambermaid at my lodging house lives across the river. She claims you have been spied there, late at night, pulling a wagon with rubber wheels."

"Keep the noise down on the cobblestones, is that it?"

"Another story from Shockoe says it's not a wagon with rubber wheels, but a rubber sack that is pulled over a victim's head."

"Suffocate 'em, I guess."

"And so their screams may be muffled?"

"Might work. But you sittin' there. I ain't no big man to do all that."

"So this rumor has no basis in fact?"

Baker leaned forward and gazed into the reporter's eyes with a new interest. The reporter met his stare, fountain pen poised above his notepad. At last, Baker relaxed into his chair, crossed his legs, and refilled his pipe.

"I ain't said that," he replied.

"They say you were stopped on the bridge hauling a body under a blanket in your rubber-wheeled wagon."

"Tell 'em he sick, gotta rush him to the infirmary at the college. Yeah, I heard that one, too."

"It's a serious accusation, sir. Murder, after all."

"So, what you think? What you tell your readers about all that?"

"Whatever you tell me, Chris. You're the only one who knows the truth of it."

"Naw, that's not what you gonna write. You gonna tell 'em the spooky stuff, the rubber wheels, the rubber sack, maybe a rubber hammer, too. Whole lotta rubber in that story, ain't it?"

"Is any of it true?"

"You want to see my wagon?"

"Do you have one, really?"

Baker shook his head dismissively, tucking the tobacco pouch back into his vest pocket. "You tell 'em what you want, say you saw it all, don't matter to me. I ain't got no rubber-wheeled wagon. I ain't got no rubber sack, nor hammer, neither. Enough stiffs in this town, you think somebody need to go makin' more? But like you say, them rumors run rife, and what you print just gonna rife up some more. People need their boogey man, you know? Boy's daddy beat him, he run away and don't come home, gotta be ol' Chris. Drunk fishin' for gar and fall in the river, ol' Chris musta got him."

"I do see what you're getting at."

"You seen this? City diggin' up that whole graveyard down poor house hill, grind the bones up for road fill, make way for a bridge over the Shockoe gorge. Ain't nobody raise a stink over that."

"I believe The Planet ran an editorial."

"He mention me in it?"

"He did, yes."

"Must be ol' Chris drivin' that steam shovel, ain't it?"

CHAPTER 19

1881

THE ONLY HALFWAY PLEASANT thing about slipping out of bed at midnight was that momentary twinge of heightened awareness for all he loved and lived for. Martha lay warm under layered quilts, the boy bundled in his crib box at her side, and the kitchen stove's glint gave the only light as he crept downstairs to the stable landing. There he bent to a cedar chest that could not quite conceal the carrion stench that permeated his work clothes. Shivering in long john pajamas, working by touch and smell alone, he donned greasy canvas overalls, two pairs of woolen socks, the high boots handed down by the Fessor Doctor and waterproofed with tallow from the lye vat, the thick sweater left by his father, a heavy leather poncho that draped past his knees, and a raccoon skin skullcap he'd fashioned himself. No scarf, they got in the way when shoveling. No earmuffs, essential to note the slightest snap of a twig. No mittens, the work required not only brute force, but dexterity.

Tipping back up the stairs, he retrieved a biscuit that Martha had left in the bread box, tossed a crumb to the cat, squatting vigilant by the guttering stove, and stepped out to a biting winter night decorated by snowflakes drifting in the gaslights of Navy

Hill. Across the city, the aggregate smoke from a thousand chimneys hung low along the rooftops, snowflakes graying as they fell. In the distance the clang and churn of the factories and the forlorn hoot of a train in the Shockoe gulch echoed. These days the teeming city never seemed to sleep. If he crept along sharp, he might slip by unnoticed, just another of the night's late workers.

Instead of his usual roundabout route through the cemetery, he braved a shorter walk down Second Street and made it to the college building without incident, finding four members of what the students had begun to call the Anatomy Society waiting by the back door, an empty bottle at their feet, another passed hand to hand. They didn't offer the bottle, of course, and Baker didn't ask. He pulled the stable door wide, awakening the ambulance horse, a black Friesian mare that could easily pull a loaded wagon. It took a half hour to harness the ambulance by lantern-light, none of the students offering to help, if they even had a clue how to do so. They laughed, stamped their feet and drank, children catching snowflakes on their tongues.

At last he spoke, giving brisk orders to the boys to grab shovels, a pick-axe, rope, a canvas tarp, and a pair of kerosene lanterns. He climbed up to the driver's seat as the students clamored in back, hooting and howling in mimicry of the haints they had not yet met or learned to respect. The ambulance turned out Franklin Street, which was just beginning to whiten along the cobblestones, and headed downhill towards the shanties in the Shockoe gulch. He looked neither left nor right, uninterested in whomever might be lurking in the shadows. A constable would have to be truly dedicated to swap a tavern toddy for a tussle in a cemetery on such a night. Anyway, the danger would be on their return, with contraband in the wagon bed, when a policeman might straggle out onto the street and wave them down.

As they climbed past the Jewish cemetery on Church Hill, a stiff wind up from the river shook the ambulance, and the horse slipped on the icy cobblestones. This graveyard he left alone, as an all-night tavern stood nearby. At the top of the hill, he turned away from the spectral St. Johns Church and its ancient gravestones of the white settlers towards his destination, the cemetery cleared from a distant grove, Oakwood. He needed three bodies in good repair for the end of term anatomy practical. One, a heart attack casualty from the upstairs infirmary, lay embalmed in the basement already. That afternoon, snow clouds gathering, he'd spied the other two, as he stood apart watching a cortege with a full brass band make its way to a knoll beneath a landmark copse of fingerling dogwoods in the colored section, then counted his steps around the hill to the rough crew of laborers who were burying their co-worker in the pauper's field. Both parties saw him, the people of the cortege pointedly turning their backs, the workers shouting curses and shaking their fists.

At the cemetery gate, he halted the ambulance behind a screen of scrub pine, instructing the greenest of the students to stand guard. The boy demonstrated a hoot owl call he'd use as a warning, and a distant owl replied. He led the other three, scowling for them to keep quiet now, through a gap in the railing, handing their tools through one by one. From this moment they were criminals, would be jailed for sure if caught inside the cemetery grounds. But all they saw around them was sifting snow, a few bare trees and the lowland dotted with the simple gravestones of thousands of young soldiers buried side-by-side, those that wouldn't fit up on Hollywood Hill. This was a dangerous spot. They would need to cross that bare plain to the pauper's field, in full view of anyone else out here on the edge of town past midnight.

Snow fell more heavily now, a lucky turn, as by morning all sign of their passing would lie buried under drifts. They crossed through the military veterans' acreage at a half-trot, then made there way down a slippery gulch towards the worker's grave, the easier one to manage, and a good place to teach the boys how to do the job right. He found the boulder he used as his compass, then told the students to follow as he paced off a count towards the grave. Even in the dark, it was easy to find, as in this part of the cemetery there were few markers, and the grave mound stood out among the other sunken plots. He'd seen them bury him head to the west, so instructed the boys to dig a narrow hole there. No use to uncover the whole grave, especially with these toothpick boxes, especially when he'd lie shallow, his crew having called it quits against the frozen creek sediment once they had the hole deep enough to drop the coffin.

He lay the tarp flat beside the grave and ordered one boy to stand clear and keep an eye out in all directions. He handed shovels to the other two, then lay the tarp out like a picnic blanket beside the grave. "Y'all put all the dirt on here, then we dump it back in when we done, and won't nobody know we was here."

The students discovered that uncovering a fresh grave, even in frozen ground, was not all that difficult. The newly turned earth gave readily to their shovels, and soon they struck wood as he'd expected, half a shovel deep. At this, he waved for the boys to back off, and with one swing of the pick-axe shattered the coffin lid. On his knees, he leaned into the hole, pulled away the pine boards, and felt for the dead man's face. The cackling that never left his ears rose to a crescendo, as he lassoed a rope under the corpse's arms, and braced himself against a ghostly pressure, as if a boot were pressing on his neck, pushing him towards the hole.

He got back to his feet, handed the rope end to the boys, ordered them to pull, and just like that, the body slid up out of the coffin, through the narrow hole they'd dug, and emerged inert onto the ground before them.

"A dead man's heavy, ain't he?" he said. "We gotta strip him, throw the clothes back in. Now fill her in good, tamp her down, and she'll look just like before". While the boys shoveled, he pulled off the dead man's ragged pajamas, all he'd been buried in, and tossed them back in the grave, then rolled the body onto the tarp, bundling it with rope.

Yes, he knew what this transgression was, like the old folks said, releasing the man's poor spirit to ceaseless wandering, now that they'd cracked the safe that held soul and body together. Sure as you're born, the stiff at his feet would join the chorus that hounded his every breath. The boys would glimpse it sometimes, too, out of the corners of their eyes. Bad luck would come to each of them in time. They knew nothing of all this, would think he was just a superstitious old crackpot if he ever let on, so he said nothing. But he noticed, as they hauled the body back to the ambulance, that all their joking had faded, all their sassy bravado shushed. Maybe they, too, heard whispers in the dancing flurries.

Snow by now beshrouded the whole cemetery, lay heavy on the pine boughs that hid the ambulance, and made walking slow work. He hurried the students along. They were cold, tired, out of whiskey, and growing disgusted at themselves, so they obeyed without complaint, eager to get the job behind them.

The second grave, he knew, was chancy. A young girl taken by the flu, daughter of the tailor who had made his suit. Baker kept a silver piece in his boot to pay off any guard the tailor might have posted, but if it was family, that wouldn't do. Only one way to find out. He led the boys back through the fence, retracing their quickly filling steps out into the graveyard, then veered uphill towards the spindly dogwood copse where the dead girl lay.

He saw a muzzle flash red just as a bullet whizzed past. They all dove face first into the snow. "You go home Chris Baker! You go home you Night Doctors!" the tailor himself shouted from the knoll. "You ain't have my daughter, you snatchers!" For good measure, the tailor fired again, sounded like an old Union carbine, that crack echoing around them. Well good for him, taking care of his kin, Baker thought, though he might catch his death of cold out here himself, and who knows, end up in a sack too before the school year was done.

"Let's go home, boys," he whispered. "We done all we can here tonight."

He stood up and shouted, "Good on you, Tailor Crawford! You guard that girl right! We done here, you done good, don't shoot again, man, don't shoot."

They crouched low, retracing their steps back to the ambulance, and turned the horse towards the college, the students in low spirits, the dead man between them on the floorboards, and Baker frustrated, wondering what to do now, one stiff short of a load. Before them, the Church Hill carriage houses and the train tracks crossing Shockoe Bottom lay purified under drifts, transformed temporarily into a pretty snow globe. The blanketed street lay empty, the only sounds the horse's muffled clopping and the creak of the wagon wheels.

At the corner of Main and 15th Streets, Baker halted the horse just long enough for the boys to jump out and slip down an alleyway at Holland's Beer Hall, where he knew they'd be met by a man well-paid by the college, who would house them in an upstairs room for the next day or two, in case they might have been seen. Back at the stable, he left the corpse where it lay in the ambulance bed, stabled the horse and cracked the ice skim in its water bucket, then went into the basement for his foraging kit. His hands and feet were numb, snow caked his beard, but what else was there to do, he had to go look, even though the odds were slim. Anybody dead before dark he'd have heard. Only chance was a fresh one gone since sundown.

Dutifully, he made his rounds, trudging straight across the old cemetery on Poor House Hill that he'd raided a dozen times already this term to the back alley of the alms house, in hopes that some consumptive soul might have coughed his last, left out in the morgue shed there. A bitter cold walk for nothing. He kept on, along the northern outskirts to the colored asylum, then south to check the rear doors of the foundling hospital and city jail, all those back streets prettified in snow but empty of human discards. Passing Dr. Watkins' house, he yearned to stop and warm himself, but feared he'd wake Martha and the baby. He stood alone in the lamplight, shaking snow from his poncho and hat. The only place he hadn't tried was the penitentiary, way down by the west side canal.

As he trudged along, he cheered himself by counting up the haul of a productive week. Already had two of the three stiffs the college needed. In addition to the man with a bad heart and the body in the ambulance, he'd retrieved an unidentified malaria victim off a steamer up from Panama, and a scalded worker from the steelworks. He regretted now sending those last two by rail to the college in Charlottesville. Take care of the Fessor Doctor first and always, he chided himself, blowing into cupped hands.

He'd been working at this pace since October, when the college term started, and was able to maintain it only because the board of visitors had the harbormaster on retainer, always on the lookout for boats beset by the tropical diseases, and because this winter's coughing flu had swept in hard. Rarely a night went by during the winter months, when he and his motley crew of students did not foray out to his old mainstays, the colored cemeteries on the north and east ends of town. Sick people everywhere of all ages. The scrofula swelled their necks like bullfrogs till they choked. They shat themselves dry with cholera or sweated out with typhoid or coughed their way to the grave with the consumption or scarlet fever. Having learned the new procedure called embalming, and having installed bunkbed-like racks along a basement wall, he could stack corpses for two weeks sometimes before they fell apart. But rarely did a body stay that long. The students could dissect a cadaver down to bone and buckets in a week. Across the long winter, roustabouts rolled whiskey barrels, each packed with a body folded like a wallet, down past the Capitol building to outgoing trains and steamships.

All that to the good, but tonight he was one stiff short, trudging through knee-high drifts down towards the river in the frigid wee hours.

At first glance, it might have been a bear. On occasion, a surly bruin would saunter into town, turning over garbage barrels and acting the fool before falling to buck shot in the street. But this time of year, bears were safely snoring away in their woody dens, so the furry mass slumped against the alley wall, caked now with snow, deserved a look. The coat was beaver pelt, and its wearer had tucked himself inside it, so it made a little igloo that even covered his feet. Maybe a tourist on a bender or out late at cards, maybe a poet drunk on absinthe, or a heartbroken swain who'd over-drowned his sorrows. Any man with a coat like that would have kin, friends, an address. White, too.

Baker hesitated before the furry tent, teeth chattering, flurries whipping up from the river and drifts swelling, as the low sky lightened towards dawn. All those winter nights across his whole life, out digging in icy rain, bitter wind, snow, yet had he ever been this cold? Or quite so deliriously exhausted? A whining in his ears grew to a clamor, gauzy shadows danced and spun about him, but it was only when the laughter came and he felt that familiar pressure at his neck, bending him towards his prey, that he surrendered and reached into his kit bag.

———————

Now to any early riser downtown, Baker himself must have resembled an old bear, what with the beaver skin coat draping the man he hauled on his back, bent double, up past the bone white Capitol building and the governor's mansion, navigating alleys among the clustered churches festooned with holiday ribbons. A mill whistle blew for morning shift, shrill in the icy air. Anything could happen now. Fortunately, snow was still falling in the gray light. His footsteps would be covered over soon. But he had to get back to the basement before someone accosted him. And then he thought, wait, everybody knows what I do. But they hate to see it thrown up in their faces, that's the real crime.

With dawn the storm dissipated, the sky cleared, and the sun rose over a city blanketed in glittering white. Bells jingled on the harnesses of sleigh-pulling horses, shovels on the cow catchers of trains pushed aside drifts, and milkmen stepped high in knee boots to reach the steps of their clients, waving at gleeful children, their noses pressed against parlor windows. In his squalid basement, Baker sat in long johns at the wood stove, lighting his father's old pipe, his feet swaddled in the dead man's furry coat. The body lay naked and curled in on itself like a newborn, on the concrete floor next to the night's other prize. Baker knew he ought to lay him out soon, before the rigor set in, but he was so beat, and just slumping there, letting the needles prick his feet and hands as they warmed, seemed all he could manage. He'd burned the man's clothes and papers in the stove. Had thrown his good pair of boots down the well. The fur coat needed to go, too, once his feet unfroze.

So much still to do. Would have to get out and shovel the walk and start the stoves in the anatomy theater before the Fessor Doctor and the demonstrator and the students straggled in. He'd have to drag out the prepared body from the rack and send it up on the dumb waiter for dissection. He needed to lay out the white man, drain his blood, and pump him up with embalming fluid. If that man's people went out looking, if someone had seen him struggling up the street beneath his heavy load, then they'd come here, he felt sure. He'd have to make up a story that would satisfy the faculty, would have to disfigure the corpse to make it unidentifiable, maybe decapitate it and throw the head in the river. Drunk fell out on the train tracks? A lot to reckon in it all. But for now the stove crackled, he could wriggle his thawing toes again, and how delicious it was to sink into a well-earned nap.

END OF THE DAY, Baker pouring slop buckets in the lye vat, when behind him he heard Professor Tompkins' voice. Man rarely came down to the basement. What was he doing here now? He set the buckets down and turned to see his employer standing with one foot on the stairs, a handkerchief raised to his nose, and the afternoon newspaper in his other hand. He didn't bother with a greeting, asking straight up, "I'm afraid you may have been seen, Chris. What did you do?"

The Fessor Doctor opened the paper to display the front page, adding, "A young man, Philadelphian, child of a prominent family it turns out, has gone missing. His friends went to the police, said they hunted for him all night in the storm."

Their eyes went to it at the same time, the fur coat bunched like a sleeping dog on the floor. "The article says he wore a beaverskin coat, Chris."

"What did they see?"

He read:

"Two burghers of Ninth Street, up early, whose names have been withheld at their request, noticed an odd apparition in the snow as night gave way to dawn, what seemed to them a bear up on its hind legs, making its way uphill towards the Capitol Building. On closer inspection and upon interrogation, both individuals concurred that this irregular image must instead have been that of a man in a heavy fur coat astride the back of another, who carried him haltingly along, knee-deep in the drifts. At the time, both imagined the end of a too lengthy night of celebration, one friend helping another to their lodgings and the morrow's headache. But upon learning of the missing Philadelphian in this morning's newspaper, each separately apprised a constable of their pre-dawn observations. As the heavy snowfall has obscured any tracks or other signs of struggle, the police captain has not been able to confirm or deny our surmise, but we do suspect that this may have been the work of the city's notorious night doctor, Chris Baker, longtime procurer of anatomy material for the Medical College of Virginia, returning with his prey to the college building. Further inquiries are underway."

Professor Tompkins folded the paper and stuffed the handkerchief into his pocket. "Chris, I never ask, but on this point I must. Was what they saw you, and the Philadelphian?"

Baker licked his mustache, and shrugged. "If it's him, he's right here, suh." He pointed at the body rack, where a pale corpse lay in repose, clearly that of a young man. A handkerchief tied around his head held his jaw shut, and pennies weighted his eyes. The body was otherwise unclothed. Baker said, "Embalmed him pretty good before class, figure he keep a week or two cold as it is."

"I must ask. Did you harm him?"

"Suh?"

"I implore you, Chris, how did you procure this corpse?"

"He 'bout froze when I come on him."

"Was he yet living then?"

Baker shrugged again, lightly toeing the beaverskin coat.

"No, do not answer," Dr. Tompkins said. He refolded the paper and turned back to the stairs, adding in a fretful voice, "Chris, you must dispose of this body, you must leave no trace, that coat, all of it must go. We will make do in dissection, do not think of that. But quickly now, attend to nothing else until this job is finished. I must go and shutter the doors, give the students a snow day, speak to the dean. The sheriff will be here, no doubt. Do not leave the building, do not go home. Dispose of that corpse, do you hear?"

Baker nodded, beginning to grasp the danger he'd skirted. He'd have to act fast.

No easy task, breaking down a fresh stiff by himself all in one go. But he hacked off the head and limbs, disemboweled the torso, and dropped all the pieces into the lye vat, stirring mightily deep into the night. As the vapors rose, they danced and murmured. Tired as he was, barely able to stand, the haints all about seemed more solid than the walls of his cell. But he soldiered on, humming along to their mournful plaints. While the dead man's flesh dissolved, he took shears to the beaver skin, throwing most of it in the well, but saving back one arm of the coat, despite his employers' demand, to make a muff for Martha. By sunrise, when the day-old snow shone fleetingly pink across the city's rooftops, his work was done. The Philadelphian had disappeared like a snowflake into a drift and a thoroughly spent Baker lay blissfully snoring on his pallet bed.

Chapter 20

Two Nights Later

HE'D NEVER in his life run short before. But the college was still down a body with practical exams on the way. Hard to believe, but his target tonight was the only colored person buried in the whole city on this day, state senator's mother caught the croup in old age, they said. Chances were, her lawmaker son would have felt protected from a grave robbing so far out, in the fenced-in, private lot at Cedarwood owned by the True Reformers Fraternal Society, would have paid dearly for it, so might have foregone the expense of a vault or a guard onsite. It was a chancy haul, clear across the Shockoe gulch, only one gate in and out, and as he harnessed the mare to the ambulance, the haints buzzed and stung at his ears more annoyingly than usual. Something was off, he sensed it, but maybe he was just so tired.

To make matters worse, the last of the snowstorm's clouds had pushed off East, leaving a clear sky and a brilliant full moon that threw long shadows across the blanketed city and painted every object in stark relief, like one of those ink sketches in a newspaper. The street had not been cleared at all. He'd have to urge the mare along in the few wagon tracks already made out to the distant graveyard, and hope she wouldn't balk. If he'd had his druthers, he'd have pushed back this adventure closer to dawn, once the moon set, but the students were acting the fool — their hideout tavern having kept them well supplied with ale — and if he waited much longer they'd be useless to follow directions. Already they were cutting up, teasing him about the newspaper article, "Callin' you fancy names now, Ol' Chris! Call you a Resurrection Man! Now, don't that have a biblical ring to it, though! Was it you, Chris? Did you murder that Yankee boy from Philly? You scary old resurrectionist you!"

As Chris turned the ambulance north towards the cemetery, along the narrow streets of the Jackson Addition, the students sitting knee to knee in the back passed their bottle and made up a song that they hooted and embellished all the way:

> *Ol' Chris the digger! He has come!*
> *And made a snatch of me;*
> *It's very hard the way he do*
> *Won't let a body be!*
>
> *Don't go to weep upon my grave,*
> *And think that there I be;*
> *Ol' Chris ain't left an atom there*
> *Of my Anatomy!*

Not a thing he could do to quiet them, would have to count on the shoveling to sober them up. He'd scouted the burial that afternoon, had seen the sturdy coffin going in a hole six feet deep. They might need to disinter the whole thing if his pickaxe wouldn't break through the lid, and this mission would have to be performed in a bright moonglow that might as well be daylight.

Chris again left the drunkest student with the horse at the cemetery gate. No use trying to hide out there under the moon.

Crusty snow gave way with a loud crunch at each step, cutting his ankles when his brogues broke through, every breath a puff of smoke like a locomotive's. It was easy to find the gravesite, the funeral attendees' footsteps making a rough trail up from the gate, and the grave itself lay piled with flowers that made a dark splotch amidst the scattered tombstones.

As he'd suspected, the old lady was laid deep. Chris spread out the tarp and carefully arranged all the flowers in their place, exactly as they'd covered the grave, then the boys went to work. They had to clear a hole large enough to stand in, shoveling dirt up to the second tarp beside the grave, while Baker waited with his pick-axe. The moon hung low by the time the boys got down to the coffin. They climbed out and fell back on the snow, exhausted, while he crawled in and punched at the casket lid with his pick-axe. Sturdy as it looked, the shellacked lid was just poplar wood and shattered easily. He bent over and tugged the bony corpse up by the shoulders, the flesh of her back sloughing off on his hands. He dropped her on the tarp, wiped his messy hands in the snow, then stripped her naked quickly, tossing her dress back in the hole.

He shrouded the rigid body, practically just a skin-wrapped skeleton, in the tarp, while the boys hurriedly refilled the grave. Thoroughly spent, they fell back against a tombstone and dozed while Chris replaced all the flowers exactly as they had been arranged on the grave mound. He'd noticed the trick, a little ribbon woven among the flowers, that the senator had placed there to detect a snatching, and made sure to replace that, too. All went well, their long shadows fingering the snowy cemetery as they retraced their steps near moonset. But there at the ambulance stood a constable in his dome hat, moonlight glinting from his rifle barrel. One of the students tossed his shovel and ran, but stopped when the policeman leveled the rifle and threatened to shoot. The other dropped the tarp-wrapped body at the officer's feet and fell to his knees, defeated. Clearly, the boy they'd left at the ambulance as their watchman had run off, and good for him. Baker strode up to the officer and asked, "So what we doin', then?"

"We goin' to the city jail is what we're doin'," the constable replied. "Looks like I got me the famous Night Doctor of Richmond, dead to rights, you might say."

"I'll be," said Baker, stepping closer. "If it ain't old Dr. Searcy. You a police now, is it?"

"And you the same old nasty body snatcher you always been," the constable sneered.

"Well, let's get on with it," Baker sighed. Searcy's rifle butt struck his temple, knocking off his skull cap. He collapsed atop the corpse and lay still, his bald head shining in the lantern light.

BAKER CAME BLURRILY AWAKE with a throb at his temple, propped in a corner of a damp stone cell. Beside him crouched the two students, their backs against the wall. Already it was clear that the other men in the cell knew who they were and why they were there. Though each had run afoul of the law separately, all stood together in the far corner, coldly eyeing the grave-robbing threesome.

"So you the one, ain't it? Call you the Night Doctor, boy," a heavily bearded, burly man called.

The boys looked to Baker for a reply, but he paid the question no mind, fishing in his vest pocket for his pipe. Had he forgotten it at home or had the jailer taken it?

"Ol' Chris!" Another prisoner growled, "How many people you dug up so far?"

Baker gingerly fingered the egg-sized bump at his forehead, glowering at the man.

"Boy cain't count, Bidie, you know that – best leave these snatchers alone," said another.

"He ain't deaf, is he? One of you fuckers is gonna answer me."

The students cowered against the stone wall. Baker's voice came hoarse, "Well, last year I'd say a good two dozen or so, for this college. Some more for the one up Charlottesville way. Some others I ain't tell."

Was he lying, playing with them? The burly man asked, "So all them bodies in just a year, you say? Chopped up by them doctors at these colleges?"

"Ain't nothin' but a butcher shop is all they is," another added.

"I hear you been manufacturin' dead bodies yourself, grabbed a man on the street just this week, drag his dyin' ass up the hill."

Baker made to stand, but that set his head spinning, so he thought better of it. Still in their crouch, the students eyed each other helplessly.

"You best leave that fool be, Connie. Spooky fucker, ain't he? I ain't mess with him."

"Shit, he ain't but a little pygmy. And look it, how y'all know he ain't took your own mama up out her grave? Strip her nekkid as a baby, all them college boys pokin' at her laid out bare to the world, chop off her titty you sucked from."

"That's my mama, boy, stop it."

"What I'm sayin', am I right? Can you prove he ain't? And you mongrels here in this cell, which of you go see the judge, he say hang, and this boy be waitin' at the scaffold, rubbin' his hands together, cain't wait."

"He's right on that, Bidie. Ol' Chris there, fast as you planted, he dig you up."

Another man added, "What them college boys do to you then, don't care what got you potted, that ain't a fair bid."

"Well here he sits, boys, the Night Doctor hisself and his little helpers, devil's own delivery man, drug up here in broad daylight like a mole dug up out his hole."

The burly man crossed the cell, kicked at Baker's boot, then bent in close, Baker daring to stare directly into this white prisoner's bloodshot eyes.

"You got a job a work, ain't you, ol' Chris?" the man said. "And you boys, chop a man up, ain't give his soul time to settle accounts and get on to the next life. No way that's right, I don't care what he done!"

Another man said, "My pal Donnie told me he come up by that old college one night, had a snort or two, and place had a chill about it, dead of summer, heard a whinin' sound, and hands was grabbin' at his throat. Liked to break his leg runnin' down that hill."

"Shoot, you won't see me up that way, day or night."

The gang by now had crept closer, all in a knot, pressing in on Baker and the students.

"That ain't the worst of it, neither. Know a boy work with Blacksmith Horner down on Canal Street, got a stomach cramp, took him up to the infirmary there. He was kickin' and screamin', no not that, no! Last Fall, October it was, ain't seen him since."

"Shit. One old man, couldn't hardly lift his head, he seen them fat columns out front, where they was haulin' him off to, he jump up and run off, anything but end up in that place."

"And you boy doctors cut on livin' people like you do the dead, ain't it?"

"We minister as we can," one student answered.

"Minister? Some minister you is, knives and saws and a bloody apron, butcher is what y'all is."

Baker said nothing, his eyes fixed on the burly man glaring just inches from his nose. At last the man stepped back, announcing, "Well, boys, we see what happens now."

The other men retreated, too, one spitting at the wall above Baker's head. "So, all them coloreds say you got the devil in your pocket. Let's see old Scratch get you out this predicament, Chris."

"Got that old snatcher dead to rights this time. Who gonna be at the graveyard, Chris, waitin' for the sheriff to cut your swingin' body down? Chop up your old black bones?"

The burly man shook his head, "You goin' to the gallows for real, Baker. Y'all get a good look at him, boys. He gon' be strung up like a Christmas goose, and I for one plan to stand out front when he swings. And you college boys? You gon' get your necks stretched, too, diggin' up old ladies out they graves."

The students sank down to the floor on either side of Baker, and hid their faces in their hands. He stretched out his legs, crossed his arms, and thought wistfully of Martha and the boy. Hated to think how she'd take all this; they'd planned a Christmas chicken.

HE NEEDN'T HAVE WORRIED. Two hours later, Baker and the students went free. The jailer reached through the bars, pointed at the three body snatchers in the corner, and called, "Y'all come now. This a new one for sure. Governor hisself walked down here this mornin' to the jail house door. Ordered me set you loose, no charges, get on home."

Baker asked the students to help him up, as the burly man shouted, "Set this fucker free?"

"Governor hisself," the jailer replied. "Walked down here on his own two feet, told me let 'em out."

Baker seemed unsurprised, like he'd expected this reprieve all along. Turning towards the door, he nodded to his cellmates. "See y'all boys," he said, pausing to scan their faces appraisingly.

The bearded man snarled, "I see you first, you catch a bullet in your teeth, boy."

Baker turned and led the students through the barred door, one of the men left behind remarking, "We just seen the devil hisself, y'all. Got the governor out of bed, he did."

As they walked down the jailhouse hallway, the jailer asked Baker, "You know who caught you, don't you?"

"Old student from the college, boy name of Searcy."

"A doctor?" one of the students asked.

"He act the fool, Fessor Doctor sent him packin'. So he's a police now. Guess he been after me a while."

"What will you do, Chris? The college needs bodies," the other student whispered.

"Y'all get on home. That old boy Searcy ain't worry me. Hey, Jailor," he asked, "you got my pipe?"

CHAPTER 21

1882

EXACTLY ONE YEAR LATER, arrested again, this time out at the pauper's section of Oakwood cemetery, collecting two end of term exam stiffs from the colored lunatic asylum, buried shallow side-by-side earlier that day. Baker and his accomplices on this venture - a student named W. D. Meredith and Caesar Roane, a down on his luck transient - all spent Christmas in jail, even went to court for arraignment (see writ next page), but the new governor, a Readjuster named Cameron, followed the example of his predecessor and set them free, no questions asked, before New Year's Day.

Interviewed by a newspaper reporter while behind bars, Baker shrugged off the untimely arrest (and the risk of a ten year jail term), allowing that the prison was warmer than his usual quarters in the college basement and that medical students had been kindly passing regular meals and even dessert cakes through the bars. He seemed unconcerned, even nonchalant about the affair, the reporter thought, telling the sobbing student Meredith not to fret.

Though he didn't mention it to the reporter, Baker's main concern was his family. He'd hoped to spend Christmas with

Martha and little Johnny up in the barn loft, warming his feet before the stove fire after exams were over. And he worried that, once again, his wife and child would be targets for derision and worse when the papers came out.

Nothing to do but wait, though, for the protections to kick in. Governor Cameron tut-tutted when Drs. McGuire and Tompkins came knocking, saying this behavior has to stop, etc., but he nodded at the college's ongoing need for cadavers. As long as it's just poor colored folks you're collecting, he advised, you go on about your business. But please tell your man Baker to be more selective about his doings, will you? This happens again, stirring the hornet's nest up in Jackson Addition, can't say what I might do.

CHAPTER 22

1883

EXASPERATED THOUGH HE WAS, when Baker got arrested again, this time hauling a body from the alms house in a wheelbarrow on the night before Halloween, Governor Cameron once again let him go. That story reached beyond state lines, including this mention in the *National Republican* of Washington, DC:

Arrest of Resurrectionists.

RICHMOND, VA., Oct. 30,—Chris Baker and William Burnett, colored men, and professional resurrectionists, were arrested, this morning while moving the body of a dead pauper through the streets on a wheelbarrow. The body had been stolen from the morgue at the city almshouse. David Parker, the keeper of the morgue, was arrested on a charge of complicity, but has been bailed. Baker and Burnett were sent to jail.

Upon hearing of Baker's release, Constable Searcy threw up his hands in frustration, pleading, "What will it take to convict this ghoul?" To which a fellow officer replied, "You best leave that man be. Here tell he put a spell on old man Cameron, make him dance a polka if he wants to."

The Interview

Baker tapped his spent pipe against a bucket on the floor to empty it, the clang stirring a voice-like echo in the little theater. It seemed that he had nothing more to say, that the interview might be ending. The reporter raised a finger, though, to ask, "When you listed the cemeteries you have visited on your rounds, sir, you omitted any of those where we whites may be interred."

"Some white folk in the potter's field, same as colored."

"Oh yes, of course that would be right. But the paid cemeteries, Shockoe Hill, Hollywood, and the white sections of Oakwood, for instance, did you never venture there?"

Baker turned the warm pipe in his palm, perhaps considering whether to refill or pocket it. At last he looked up and studied the reporter closely. He asked, "That ain't a serious question, is it?"

"What do you mean?"

"Would I be sittin' here talkin' to you, if we'd ever gone in them graves?"

"Ah."

"And even if we ever did dig in them white graveyards, tellin' you 'bout it ain't the wisest thing a man can do, is it? Bad enough got the whole colored city down my neck. But the boss man's who run this town, long as you stay out their graves, they fine with whatever else I got to do. Daddy taught me that, and he knew y'all white folk pretty good."

CHAPTER 23

PRICE'S FUNERAL HOME

FUNERAL DIRECTOR PRICE had hired a youngster to fend off the salesmen who pestered his doorway all day long, but this vendor he had invited in, all the way from Baltimore, and welcomed him to his office, though he did pause and reconsider for a moment at the door. The man's attire was ridiculous. Why these northern peddlers had taken to broad-paned checkered suits, he could not say. Did they not grasp how their mawkish get-ups only mirrored their claims for products no one needed and that rarely repaid purchase price, if anyone suckered for them at all?

But this shyster knew his mark, clearly, and despite his clownish outfit, adopted an indifferent tone, as if not at all sure that this Southern town deserved the advance his invention promised. Price settled into his chair, clipped and lit a cigar, and waited for the man to speak. There seemed to be no hurry.

At last the salesman asked, "So, you inquired about protection?"

"Ah, he speaks! Well, yes, I think you may have heard of our situation here?"

The salesman smirked, as if the thought were beneath him, replying, "Resurrectionists, is it?"

"You may bequeath them that honorific. We say body snatchers, in the vernacular."

"Grave robbers."

"That, too. Too much of it of late. The Medical College has its needs."

"We have those schools in Baltimore, too."

"Plus, there is talk of yet another institution of doctoring coming to Richmond. Our constituents clamor for a solution, which is why I sent the telegram."

"Yes, well, what have you tried so far?" the salesman asked. "I understand that some of your brethren are holding back bodies a whole week, even in Summer, burying them only after the corruption has set in, as a stay on the snatcher's interests?" He twisted in his chair and took an obvious sniff of the pine-scented air.

"Not here at Price's. We treat the dead here with decorum and dispatch. But we do seek a more tenable solution."

"Indeed, and a solution is in store." The salesman lifted a heavy ring-bound notebook from his valise and pulled from it a brochure. Emblazoned across the front were the words:

Rest in Peace, not in Pieces! Mort-safes will guard your departed in the tomb awaiting their Heavenly Call!

"Mort-safes, you call them."

"Yes, and safe they are! Rust-proof steel cages, fit to any coffin, pediatric or adult. Our cage design has been approved by the Roman Pope himself, not all-encasing, as a vault might be, allowing, as you may assure your grieving clients, the heaven-bound soul to escape through its bars in due time, but maintaining the body untouched until the Day of Judgment itself, when soul and body reunite to face the Lord in glory. Not, as they rightly fear, damned to all eternity. Lost and wandering wraiths. In futile search of their visceral parts. Snatched and scattered by some ghoul."

"Mort-safe, you say," Price repeated. "Will you have a cigar, then?"

"Indeed, yes sir. Upon receipt of your telegram, can have the item manufactured to your specifications, on a train and at your depot, in three days, that is our guarantee."

"Mourners may balk at the expense."

"We do offer an accessory plan, a funeral insurance at a nickel a month, if you may be so inclined."

"Oh no, that area is well covered in these parts, or shall be. We are in discussions with the new penny bankers about just such a funeral insurance."

"Then, shall we proceed? Allow me to send a standard size sample immediately to your door at our cost. You can be sure, no body snatcher will resurrect a corpse defended by our patented Mort-Safe. This, too, our guarantee to you."

"Will you be meeting with others in the trade on this visit?"

"You are our first and exclusive client in the Richmond area. On your handshake, sir, I grant you a six month's head start on the pack, amongst the colored undertakers. After that time, the fame of our arrangement will have spread, and as you surely understand, I must then bow to demand."

"Six months? Make it a year and we have a deal."

"You do recognize, however, that once the white complected undertakers of Richmond learn of our arrangement, they will very likely insist. Though, of course, this will in no way impinge upon your trade!"

"Oh yes, the stained glass artists did a great business here-abouts once they saw my windows."

"Exactly my thought. Please do take these additional brochures to share with your penny bankers, will you? We would be happy to help them in drawing up funeral insurance riders, too, should they ask."

Price nodded, releasing a smoke ring from his pursed lips. "An ironic twist, is it not, that the very body snatchers we revile may be the making of a new profit in our enterprise?"

The salesman stood and offered his hand. "Indeed, sir. If there were no diggers, we might need to invent them ourselves."

Chapter 24

1885

Summoned to Dean Taylor's office, five students from the class of '86 stood together in a line before his desk, all wearing hang dog expressions. The white-bearded professor rose from his chair to address them, assuming a martial stance and allowing his gaze to scan each of their callow faces one by one. At last he commanded, "Which of you will speak to this incident?"

The boy in the middle, son of one of Taylor's old classmates, now practicing in Alexandria, coughed, and raised his head to meet the professor's piercing gaze. "We were all just glad to have him back, sir. Feared he might be jailed for good this time."

Taylor allowed a stiff nod and a second student, a local boy from St. Paul's, added, "Ol' Chris, he was sweeping the vestibule when the Grover Cleveland parade went by, all of us out on the steps to see it, having a smoke, it wasn't any planned thing at all, honestly, sir."

"You were all," Taylor said, his eyes narrowed. "Other than the five of you, who else would you say?"

"It was us," the Alexandrian replied, "maybe one or two others from the first years, I don't know, it was a crowd out there."

"And so?"

The local student turned to his comrades, none of whom seemed interested in speaking up, and added, "A lot of election signs, people in the parade passing out torches, band was loud, seemed like the whole city was in on this parade, it was a celebration, really, sir, about filled the whole street. Did you see it?"

"I have heard. But to your point."

"Well, sir, I can't say who was the first or the second either, it all flew up pretty quick, but next thing we know we're caught in the mix, and somebody, I don't know which of us, grabs ol' Chris and pulls him into the parade, somebody lights his broom off a torch, and it's waving in the air, we're all arm-in-arm, him in the middle of us, and I don't know how but some way we ended up right in front of the band, all marching together."

"You led the parade. Oh my." Taylor sighed deeply, conjuring the scene. "Baker went willingly?"

"Well," the Alexandrian said, "truth be told, at the start he pushed back, begged us not to drag him out there."

A third student, a stocky boy in round glasses, raised a finger at that, adding, "If I may Professor, we all feel pity for Chris, locked up in his dungeon like he is, thought it might do him good to get some fresh air, is all."

"Fresh air? Has it occurred to any of you swains that Baker may have good reason to avoid this fresh air you speak of?"

For a long moment no one spoke, then the local boy sighed, "We do now, sir, yessir."

Professor Taylor rubbed his forehead and looked away, at last asking, "Will one of you please explain how it happened?"

The stocky boy answered, "Well sir, the parade turned onto Broad Street, and everything was fine, really, everybody in high spirits, passing bottles and all, and if I may sir, Chris too seemed, at that moment, wouldn't you agree boys, he was cheered, I think, to be out on a spring day in broad daylight amidst the people?"

"He was waving his flaming broom," a fourth boy added.

"We didn't think it was...." The fifth student, a willowy type, allowed.

"Exactly," Professor Taylor said, pointing a finger at one and then the other down the line. "You, none of you, cared to think."

"No sir, we did not," mumbled the local boy.

"And then what?" the doctor asked, pacing now behind his desk.

The stocky boy continued, "Well, sir, the parade started to peter out a little down around Second Street, aimed to turn up in the Jackson Addition, and you know the crowd gets a bit darker up that way, and that's when ol' Chris started to get upset."

The Alexandrian added, "He dropped his broom, fire was out anyway, and then he just broke from us, and ran."

"Did you follow?"

"We did sir."

"And?"

"Well sir, Chris, bless his heart, he only took a dozen steps before they caught him. Man grabbed his coat tail, then a gang of colored fellows went for him, and I just, what could we do?"

"You witnessed this beating? And did nothing?"

No one replied, all resuming their hang dog posture.

Taylor asked, "Well, then when the police broke it up, and brought him to us, where were you then?"

Again, no reply.

"Am I to understand that you rejoined the parade? All of you, and the others you do not care to name?"

"It was a riot, sir, I mean at the time, what could we do?" the stocky boy pleaded.

"Broken ribs, both eyes blacked, spitting blood, his torso one continuous bruise. They all but killed our man. And you did nothing."

"Can we see him, sir?" the local boy asked.

"He convalesces away from the college, in a secure location, with family, is being looked in on. He will heal in time. But you, all of you, we should have you expelled."

Professor Taylor again raked an accusing glance along the row of chastened faces.

"Go now. Ponder this. And for God's sake, as future physicians, learn to think before you act, will you? The Grover Cleveland parade. Of all things."

Plainly disgusted, Taylor waved the students away and sank down in his chair. Alone again, he sat listening to a distant just-human shrieking, no doubt some poor injured soul in the infirmary downstairs. Chris Baker might have been killed, he thought. The students had behaved like idiots. But really, they are not the ones to blame. If we are honest, it is this institution and its needs, its demands. We own that poor man's wounds.

BAKER LABORED UP THE STAIRS, leaning heavily on his wife, his eyes so swollen they were nearly shut. She led him to their bed and propped him upright with pillows, so he could breathe more easily, then brought him a cup of broth she'd seasoned with wild scallions.

He sipped at the broth, his breath shallow, saying nothing. She sat at his side, holding back her many questions. Their son peered over the foot of the bed; she'd shushed him not to speak. Maybe it was his wheezing, but in the quiet arose an odd nattering sound, and a dim shriek of some kind behind it. "Our own kind done this to you," she whispered. "Oh my husband, why they hate you so?"

Chapter 25

Tate's Barber Shop - Jackson Ward - 1887

"Boys, I plugged that fucker not ten feet away, right up there on Hospital Street."

"With that gun you got, that old Yankee revolver?"

"Listen. Bullet turn around in the air, is all I can figure."

"Get out this shop, Ronnie, with that fool talk."

"I got the gun right here. Looka this." He bent to retrieve a long-barreled Colt revolver from his satchel and held it out balanced in his palm.

"Son, put that piece away! Sheriff walk by see that!"

"Naw, look, take this gun. Now, site down the barrel. Is it true?"

"A fine piece, I will say that."

He took the weapon back, gripped it in both hands, arms extended, and crouched by the coat rack. "I laid in wait for that devil out at the Sycamore graves, figured he be up there scoutin' the funeral for that Thomas girl died of the red rash, and sure 'nuff, here he come struttin' out the front gate like he own the place. I tell you, boys, he one proud little fucker, ain't he? But I know to my soul he got my papa, and some a y'all else in here done lost loved ones to them night doctors, am I right? Governor cut the boy loose, but here I am gon' shoot the fucker in broad daylight of a Tuesday afternoon and who you think stop me?"

"Put that piece away, now, Ronnie. Stop playin' in here!" The barber left his patron and went to the window, closing the louvered shades, so bars of sunlight striped the checkered floor. "You be wearin' them stripes you keep this up," he warned.

"I tell you boys, popped that fucker point blank in the chest, close as that chair right there." He triggered the gun from his crouch and all heard it click. He stood then, offering the gun around, but no one took it, though none took their eyes from it either.

"This barrel straight and true, y'all see that? But what I'm sayin' is... Bullet...turn...around ...in the air. Come whizzin' past me, broke a window in the tannery back behind."

The barber returned to his patron, shaking his head. "Hit the wall and ricochet is what."

"Weren't no wall behind him. Wall behind me!"

"Yeah, what Baker do?" the man in the chair asked.

"He stop, see me pointin' this gun, and lay down that stare like his eyes was blind or seen right through me, little bit of a evil grin under that old mustache a his, and boys, call me cuckoo but I seen bats, bats in broad daylight come up flappin' out his coat, and you know what? They laughin' at me, they laughin'!"

"Laughin' bats now, you say? Gone a step beyond with that one," the barber laughed. "Put that piece away, Ronnie. Last time I tell you. You dreamed all this shit, son."

"Dream, my ass, wide awake as you standin' there. Ain't no fuckin' ricochet neither."

"Stick my 12-gauge upside his head, he ain't turn around no buckshot," a waiting patron replied.

"Somebody gotta do somethin' is what I say."

"What we gon' do? Governor hisself under his command."

"Look, your own brother make barrels for him, pack up

them bodies for the train. He pay cash on the barrel head for 'em, too."

"So now you blamin' my brother, is it?"

"I ain't blamin' nobody, Skip. Man go 'round lettin' off pistols in broad daylight, he end up in the graveyard hisself. And then Ol' Chris get you for sure," said the barber.

"Naw, thing we gotta do, we gotta all go in on killin' this man, cain't be just one of us takin' pot shots all the time."

"You be careful what you say, now."

"Wait, that's correct is how I see it", a waiting patron replied. "Baker just one man, even if he do have protection about him."

"But you cain't go stormin' into that old college in a mob, police wrap us up tight we try that."

"What about this, then, ambush the little fucker?"

"Jimmy, lock the door now. Y'all hush."

"What you sayin', Ronnie?"

"Sayin' we stake the place out, he cain't stay in there forever. My cousin's boy a valet for one of them doctor students, he can find out when they low on bodies, need to go get one, right?"

"Take four or five of us, and hell, all the family he dug up, prob'ly get two dozen shooters in a finger snap, we axe around."

"You got that right. Pop a hole in that grave robbin' fucker."

"Yeah, so, just for example, Skip here stake out the front door out by them columns, Buddy get the back door by the stable, he come out we blow a whistle or somethin', alert the rest of us."

"But we cain't bunch up in a gang, police call that a mob, and we all hang."

"Naw, that's the trick of it, see. One man to a block, have a gun ready. Blacksmith's on Marshall, get up on that roof. 'Nother man down the hill at the colored school. I put up at the Monument Church, and you down by the old White House, everybody spaced out like we takin' the breeze."

"I see that, yeah. And then wait, let him pass, get out the shadow of that old Egyptian monstrosity, go on his rounds."

"Get 'im when he come back. Yeah."

"Just light into him, is what we do. He cain't get away, got him cornered any which way he go."

"See if can turn all them bullets."

"I will say this," the barber allowed, "man finally get him, be a hero all down the Jackson Addition."

"And look, police hear them shots, we just melt away. Nobody say nothin'."

"Somebody say somethin'. Killin' that man front page news. All you fools hang behind that one."

"And look, it ain't Baker, he just the hand in it all. Them doctors and students the ones, chop a man's leg off you go in with a scratch. They's the one needs a bullet."

"Shit boys, you got to stop all this fool talk. Crackers get wind of this, come up here and torch this place. Any of y'all get out of it still got a head on your shoulders, who gon' cut your hair then?"

"Naw, we ain't killin' no white man, least not with no gun."

"Wife slip a little gris gris in a soup bowl maybe."

"Yeah, like that judge keel over last week, what they call it, apoplexy, was it?"

"A lotta that ol' apoplexy goin' round."

"Hear tell ol' Baker might a played a hand in that, too."

"See, what I'm tellin' you! Y'all don't know all that man's about. How many times he been shot at, he still walkin'?"

"You say that, barber, 'cause you ain't had your mama dug up and splayed out nekkid to the world, them boys slicin' at her like a Christmas turkey."

"I got this razor you say my mama again. You don't know shit, boy."

Ronnie stepped over to the dental shelf and lifted a jaw bone missing its molar teeth. He turned back to the others and waved the jaw for emphasis: "We got to kill that man is what I know."

"Take this conspirin' somewhere else then. It ain't come back on me," the barber said, snatching the jaw away.

"Alright, fine. Look, I know all you men got guns. Diggin' season's on us, too, them doctor boys always come back when the weather change. Who got a sick mama, a sick grandma, might not last the winter? What you say now, boys?"

CHAPTER 26

BAPTISM SUNDAY - 1892

"MR. BAKER, don't you look the dapper gentleman this morning!"

"Do I, now? Still got the stink about me?"

"You smell like a lily of the valley, sir. That rose soap has done you good."

Baker reached for his felt bowler, placed it atop his balding head, and called to their son, already dressed in knee breeches and a short-waisted jacket. Martha, in her daisy-print dress and wide-brimmed hat decorated with fresh daisies from the pasture, was spring itself. They stepped out the stable door, arm in arm, on an April day alive with bird song on their way to church.

He'd tried to talk her out of it. The First African Baptist Church had been her worship place since childhood, its congregation the cream of the city, so anybody who didn't know already would see that they were a couple, which meant that all the trials he faced in daring the daylight would come down on her, and on the boy, too, he feared. But the dear woman was so innocent and good that she couldn't be made to see that, even when he reminded her of the beating, showed her his overcoat, stuck a finger through a bullet hole in its sleeve. She'd had this idea all along, of course, begged his courage and swore that all would be well. Adding that, this day accomplished, they might in time afford a church wedding, their bond thereby certified in the eyes of the Lord and the community, too.

But as they turned onto Broad Street, he pulled them close. Parishioners in carriages paused to look askance, then clucked to their horses. Bowler hat or no, lovely wife or not, even with a child at their side, they knew Baker for what he was and made their signs. Martha took a seat on a long bench near the church door, in case things did not go well. Every worshiper who entered noted their presence and steered clear. A busy day with a visiting minister up from Raleigh, a rousing orator famed even in the old days for his rhetoric. They'd split his tongue to shut him up, but sewn together again, he lisped, and in that slit-stitched lisp ulterior voices whispered. No one would miss this sermon. Baptismal Sunday, too.

Though the church was soon crowded to the rafters, no one shared their bench. Martha missed none of it, sitting erect in her flowered bonnet, son fidgeting at her side. But she smiled with relief when Maggie arrived on the arm of her husband Armstead, whose team of carpenters and bricklayers had built half the homes in the Jackson Addition. They paused at the doorway to survey the congregation, she in a blue satin gown that swept the floor, languidly waving that silk and ivory fan she'd ordered from Japan. And then with a regal shrug, she pointed away from their usual seat near the altar, instead taking the one empty pew beside her friend and the man she'd chosen, giving a quick pinch to the boy's cheek, now y'all say a word about that.

So this is the day, Baker mused. He'd spent his whole life in the shadow of this church, the sprawling brick edifice looming at the height of Broad Street just around the corner from the college building. He'd seen crowds arrive and depart, nearly every day of the week, often white folk, too, debating this or that. He'd stood by that back window in the shade and listened to the congregation singing, but had never dared to darken its door. This was all for Martha. What her gracious friend Maggie was up to, he couldn't say.

For this occasion, Martha had stepped away from her seat in the choir stall, knowing she could not leave her man alone on the pew. She nodded a silent thanks to dear Maggie, who returned a brief reassuring smile. What was poor Chris feeling, she wondered? Discomfort, surely, at the judging gaze of the congregation, embarrassment at finding himself inside the sanctuary on this momentous morning, but why his trembling? Her fingers entwined his, holding him there, as she recalled that fateful day when she'd found him soaked and muddy, sprawled on his father's grave. Every step of their way since had been cautious, defiant in the face of the community's ire, and colored by incident. She had heard the people around her hiss all the names as she passed: goblin, ghoul, snatcher, devil, even cannibal. Maggie, she thought, was the only person of the thousand and more in the church on this morning that she could truly call a friend.

Their minister, old Reverend Holmes, stepped to the pulpit for his invocation, his gravelly voice hushing the worshippers. Martha bowed her head and silently prayed for help to calm her husband's trembling. But as they all rose for the first hymn, and the pastor called for the newly saved to come get their baptismal robes, she saw that he could not stand, as if pinned to his seat. She crouched to him and touched his cheek, but he didn't seem aware that she was there. That same boy in the graveyard that day.

"Come, Chris," she pleaded, "please."

Her voice, as always, brought him back. He squeezed her hand, patted his son's knee, and stood to join the others in the changing room.

CHAPTER 27

MONDAY MORNING - EXCHANGE HOTEL

"THAT FOOL AIN'T NO MORE SAVED than a cur on the street! What he do call hisself gettin' baptized? And inside the church sanctuary, too!"

The two cooks in identical aprons stood opposite each other at a long bakery table, shaping dough for the Exchange Hotel's famous breakfast biscuits. A flour-dusted square of dough as wide as the table lay before them, and with all four hands they pressed the rounded edges of tin cans into the dough and deftly twisted out precision circles, working towards the center where their efforts would expertly converge. Biscuit-making came second nature to them. They could mix and shape and bake in their sleep, all while roundly reviewing the notable events of any weekend.

"It's that Maggie's doin's, she always lookin' after her little Martha. And that poor girl, took up with that body snatchin' beast. No good in all that! Was you there?"

"Oh you know that, baptism Sunday make for a long day, but I will not miss it, 'less I'm laid up in bed. They's a spirit in the church them days like no other, ain't it, you 'bout feel the Lord's breath and angel wings flappin', all them souls reborn up out the baptismal pool. But me, I knowed somethin' was up the minute I set my pew. Now you can blame the weather, storm brewin' up the river like you get of a hot July, and it ain't barely spring yet, flowers still on the forsythia bushes, but somethin' was off, I can tell you that right now.

"Still, we got through the guest sermon and the Lord's Supper alright, then Pastor went out to get his wadin' robe on, while the choir sang 'I Surrender All' like they do. That's when I noticed, Martha won't up in the choir loft, she was settin' next to Miz Walker, that boy between 'em. You know my niece Cherisse was up for baptizin' this time, sweet child got the call at that January revival, preacher in from Tennessee with that catch in his throat? They was two dozen lined up in they robes and she innocent as the child she is, ain't even know what a sin is, but want to give her all to Jesus, bless her sweet soul, and Lord, as my eye passed down the line, Old Man Palmer back again, must be his third or fourth time through – people say he get baptized just for the bath – and then, oh my, it's like the whole congregation seen it at the same time, you could hear people catch they breath all around.

"That's why Martha come out the choir! Chris Baker hisself in line for a baptism! I 'bout fell out my seat. Well, alright, I say, Lord do mighty work in mysterious ways, but you tell me what Black man got a darker spot on his soul than that fool? I ain't even like to speak his name. Now Pastor step into the pool all normal, it ain't bother him, so alright. And ain't it a pretty sight the way he do, take they hand they come down the pool steps, all them gas lamps flickerin' so the light in the water dance all around they face, I call it angel kisses, and they so solemn, he hold his hand up say his little prayer, and then back they go in the pool! That's what I love, when they come up again, saved to the Kingdom, do all them crazy things. Shout hallelujah! Spittin' and catchin' they breath, eyes squeezed shut and then pop wide like they been on a long journey and come back reborn. Oh, I would never miss that!

"Little Cherisse, when she go, she calm as can be, come up out the water serene as she went in, Lord ain't have much work to do over her. And then, this what you want to know, Chris Baker's turn. I cut my eyes down Maggie way, and that Martha, she prayin' up a storm, huggin' that boy so he squirm, her eyes shut tight. Baker put his foot on the pool step, and no lie, right then the storm come. It was a hard rain hit the roof like the flat of a hand!

"Baker ain't but a little man, and bald as a doorknob. But to think what he do! He come down the ladder hisself, and wade into the water, and the man so short, you could just see his pecan head over the ledge. Then, oh my, girl! You ask anybody was there, somethin' like a caul fall over the sanctuary, gas lights go out, look like a shadow come through the door. Made my mouth go dry, taste of tin in my throat, and BOOM! I tell you that thunder bolt hit somewhere close. You just know was the Lord God hisself clap His Mighty Hands, NO!"

"Reverend Holmes about to tip ol' Chris down when it struck, he come up flailin', never did get down in the water good, elbow caught the Preacher upside the jaw and flip him right out the pool! Congregation go crazy then. Shoutin'. Throwin' down hard. And Baker, he roll up out the basin, fall on the floor shakin' like a fish on the river bank, spin around on his back, robe all up around his neck like he was fightin' it. Deacon come over, took a kick in the shin. Then this is what got me, a sight I never wished to see, and now cannot get out my poor skull, that little man roll over on his hands and knees. Now some people say they heard it and some don't, it was a commotion in the place, but I seen Baker rear up and cut loose with a howl like a old bobcat caught his leg in a trap. Yes he did. And then, if that ain't devil enough, Preacher layin' flat out on the carpet like he dead, knocked out cold he was, and now Baker come crawlin' on all fours, fast too, like his ass was on fire, right down the middle aisle. Ushers seen him comin' with that head a steam, they just throw open the double doors and step aside.

"And then he gone. But what a ruckus he left behind!

"Martha, oh poor Martha, what she mess with that fool for? She jump up, now it her turn to cut loose with a cry, leave her own son on the pew with the Walker's, out that door after her man she go, rain and lightnin' and thunder and all. I tell you if a herd a goats come through that church, wouldna made the mess that fool did. Preacher sit up, look around like his head on backwards, people up out they seats like they seen a ghost, or worse'n that, you ask me. Still got two to baptize, but ain't no way they gettin' in that water, uh uh. We all just left that place, prayin' Dear Lord Jesus all the way home I did, let the rain soak me down, let it come, Lord cleanse my soul of what I seen on this day. Way it look to me, even Jesus Christ cain't abide that nasty heathen."

CHAPTER 28

HOW IT WENT FOR CHRIS

HE DIDN'T HEAR the clap of thunder or feel the church shake. He didn't know his body seized, didn't hear himself bellow, didn't realize that he had spun from the basin, fallen onto the floor, and lay convulsing, a babble of nonsense syllables pouring from his frothing mouth. He saw instead a pageant playing out across the congregation, as one by one the people in the pews dissolved to bone in their Sunday best. Vapors rose from their veiny skulls and converged about him, jabbering and nagging. This was not just the usual teasing feints and jabs at his elbows as he carved flesh away from bone, not the echoing laughter that accompanied his stirring of the lye vat, or that insistent pressure, like a foot on his neck, that he had come to expect when pulling a corpse from a grave, this was an animal force that grabbed him by the throat and threw him to the floorboards.

He came to himself again on the pallet in the basement of the college, surrounded by all his wooden figurines. The baptismal robe lay on the floor in ruins, torn at the seams, soaked in sweat and urine, and the bed clothes rank with vomit. He had been lying there sobbing for who knows how long, and at his side, his dear Martha, her eyes forever changed.

He sat up at last, her presence shocking him. "No, you cain't be down here! This ain't a place for you!" he cried.

Behind her the chamber door stood open. She had come down the stairs, he knew, had seen the bottled half-borns lining the wall, had fought past the horrible stench of the bubbling lye vat, the tall stack of bones, the rotting corpse on the butcher block dripping to the slop buckets, and the cats gnawing entrails in the corner.

"Oh, Chris, oh Chris," she was saying. "That poor woman on the table – I knew her, Miz Perkins, she used to do laundry with me!"

Crowding the opposite corner, laughing uproariously, so he could hardly hear his wife's startled words, leered the thing that had been shadowing him all these years, at last revealing itself in broad daylight, a mish-mash monster with ogling eyeballs atop a many-armed body ringed with grinning skulls, all balanced atop furry legs tapering down to cloven hooves.

"Now I see you," Baker whispered, trembling.

A hundred eyeballs whipped about, straining towards him on their stalks. *'Bout time, too,* the monster's belly mouth guffawed. *Been seein' you, boy!*

CHAPTER 29

AT MAGGIE WALKER'S HOUSE

Mrs. Walker saw her friend trembling at her 3rd Street gate, that pretty yellow dress damp and sagging, her hat ruined. The storm had moved off downriver, and behind it left a chill. Summer and Winter bookending a day of early Spring. She called the boy over, and he lifted his little hand to wave. That seemed to give her friend the courage needed to open the gate.

First things first, help Martha change into something dry, get some soup in her, see that her son's alright, then, Lord willing, maybe the words would come.

CHAPTER 30

WEDNESDAY ON THE RIVER

MARTHA SAT WATCHING HER SON, who was crouched on the river bank, poking mud with a stick. She let her thoughts churn along with the frothy brown rapids at their feet. This was the bench where she and Chris had lingered on that fateful summer Sunday, where she'd talked him into what he most wanted, and busy as their work was, she with her laundresses, and he at the college, they'd done alright. She'd lost friends, knew people talked, and yes, she had salved his bruises, and had seen his finger worm through that bullet hole in his coat. But somehow, she had not ever let herself picture in her mind's eye what his job entailed. So horrible, she found herself repeating, though her lips hardly moved.

It had to be the storm, she thought. Like that night in the cemetery. She'd felt him tremble beside her in bed when thunder showers passed along the river. Bad timing to hold a baptism on a stormy day. But what was that in his eyes? He'd looked at her, looked through her, really, almost like he was blind.

It would not come easy. She told the swirling river that, in all honesty, it might never come. Now that she'd seen it herself.

Now that she'd gagged and retched and recoiled at his touch. The things they called him were simply names for the truth. Of course, he was despised, of course, they were out to get him, of course, all of it.

When they'd furnished their rooms, when he'd first loaded wood in their kitchen stove, and they'd dined by the window, then he had seemed so gentle and at peace. On the rocker by the wood stove, dozing. How she'd slip the spent pipe from between his lips.

And then there was what Maggie had said that afternoon, like what she'd seen in the basement, all so confusing. Her dear Armstead had taken the boy out back, and set to teaching him how to hit a can with a slingshot pebble. She had huddled in one of Maggie's silk robes by the fireplace, sipping tea from a china cup. For the longest time, Maggie just held her hand, saying nothing, allowing her thoughts to settle.

At last, though, she asked, "Were you there the Sunday I was baptized?"

"Must have missed it, Maggie, I'm sorry. Why you ask?"

"We didn't know each other then. I was little. But your husband is not the first person to jump out of the baptismal pool and run wild out the front door."

"Did you?"

"Oh yes. And in those days, you won't believe it, I was shy as a mouse. But something took me in the waters. Mother found me down by the turning basin, blocks away, tears of joy and salvation yet running down my cheeks!"

"Well. Yes. But that is not...."

"Martha, something I should have told you. Should have long ago. I've known your husband my whole life."

"What? How is that? He never said. Why didn't you...."

Maggie took the empty cup from Martha's hand.

"My suspicion is that he hasn't made the connection

between the little girl next door and the grown woman I am now."

"Next door? What do you mean?"

"My home. I grew up in lodgings directly behind the Medical College, in the afternoon shadow of that old tomb, we used to call it. My mother whaled me good one time for daring to stray across the street to play between the fat columns of its portico!"

"You did what?"

"As you do now, we lived above a stable, but that barn held the college's ambulance and its dray horse. Many nights in the winter, I'd awaken to the sound of that wagon going and coming. We all knew why and where it went."

"The graveyard."

"I would climb from bed and creep to my window. Have seen him, your husband, haul the dead across the street to the back door of the college, their bodies sprawled across his back, many a time."

"You poor child. A nightmare."

"If only I could have convinced myself of that."

To collect herself, Martha stood and went to the back window, where she watched her son and Maggie's husband gathering pebbles for their game.

Maggie said, "There's more."

Martha pulled the robe close around her waist and took her seat again. The ghastly expression of the dead woman, an acquaintance, her poor old bony body splayed on the butcher block. The fat cats, the dripping, the darkness, the deathly odor.

Maggie said, "Do you remember when we first met, at the Powhatan Hotel, when you were helping my mother with laundry?"

"Yes, of course. My first paid work. So grateful to her."

"Well, she knew the man who would be your husband, had a deal with him as long as she worked, bless her soul."

"A deal? What kind of deal?"

Maggie allowed a considered breath before asking, "Where do you think her soap came from?"

"Soap?"

"We shared food from our garden plot and from berry picking, and for that your Mr. Baker made us laundry soap in trade. We never saw him in daylight. He would come just before my bedtime, to the foot of the stairs, and call up to us. Mother would go down with a basket of food and return with bars of lye soap. I would watch from a crack in the door. We always thought, such a curious fellow. And then to see him again, at your side!"

"You never said. Why didn't you say?"

"This is a small town, when you think of it, Martha, wouldn't you agree? Everybody knows everything. It didn't seem of consequence. Until today."

"Why are you telling me this now?"

"Because I know what you saw there. When Mother chased us inside, well, you know that only piqued my curiosity. The next day I went back, dared to push open the basement door just a crack. I have seen."

"But Maggie! It's so awful!"

"My dear friend, buck up, will you? How can you not have guessed?"

"Oh my, what will I do?"

"I can't tell you that. Don't know what I'd do. I don't condone your man's work. The desecration of graves. What those doctors do to learn their trade. You're like my big sister, Martha, how can I advise you anything? But that man, Chris Baker? I saw it in his eyes when I peered down the stable stairs all those years ago. Watched him stir that pot. But for you and your boy out back, that man is the loneliest soul on earth. And what you have learned, in all its ugliness, is why. So his burden is yours, too, now. But it doesn't have to be just the two of you. I said all this because I want you to know that I'm in on your secret, have been all along, and that yet you and I are friends."

Friends. What kind of friend would keep a secret like that? Martha wondered. She called her son over, worries tossing like a leaf in the troubled rapids at her feet.

"What is it, Mama?" the boy asked. "Why you cryin'?"

She took her son's sleeve, smudged with mud, and began to rub it with her knuckles. Her voice came out in a whisper, with a wisdom that surprised her. "You know, Johnny, one thing a life in the laundry will teach you, some stains take work. Some won't lift no matter how much elbow you put into it. But some you think are in for good, if you let it sit a while, soak, then scrub hard with some bleach. You never know, though, until you plunge that old rag in the soapy water, which way it will go."

CHAPTER 31

DR. WATKINS' BACKYARD

BY THE END of the week, Reverend Holmes had heard enough. He made his way on foot to Navy Hill, conferred with Dr. Watkins at his door, then walked back to the barn. He found Mrs. Baker in the backyard, hanging the doctor's linens on a line, and stood there in his Sunday suit, awaiting her notice. What a precious woman, in the bloom of her youth, lithe and fluid in her movements, a wonder to behold. Only when all the sheets were hung and limply waving in the breeze did she acknowledge her visitor. She turned away from the line, briskly clipped a clothes pin to her apron, and stood there, at a distance, eyeing him.

"Martha," Holmes said, removing his hat and setting himself like he was ready to preach.

"Can I help you, Pastor?" she replied, holding her ground at her wash basket.

"Martha," the preacher began, "I have known you since before you got your milk teeth. Came to your home and gave you your name, bought many a game bird from your father. We go back your family and mine. But sugar, we can't have these acts of unruly possession in our church, that's not what we're about. This is the mother church of the South, the altar of a good God and Shepherd who loves and guards our way."

Back-dropped by the sheets, she crossed her arms, saying nothing, though her brow was creased above narrowed eyes.

He pressed his case, "Now I can't say that I have never felt the spirit move amongst us, have myself fallen out on occasion when the oratory reached its crescendo. My own dear wife has suffered fainting spells on a warm Sunday under the perorations of a visiting minister. We allow all that. But this occurrence, unprecedented, upsetting. I won't abide it. The itinerant preachers won't come, it disrupts their flow. People have been at my door all week saying it's up to me to stop it, so as much as it pains me, I had to come here."

Even from across the yard, Martha could make out the minister's purpled cheek, where the elbow had caught him. At last she said, "You had to come here, but you didn't go there, to speak to Mr. Baker himself?"

"Martha, you know I can't do that."

"You think what he do is some low-down dealings you can't abide, is that right?"

"Martha, I..."

"You and your pulpit around the corner from the college where that boy was born and raised and you never spoke to him, you never acknowledged he was alive, and of all the people in this whole broken city, who need you more than him?"

"Martha, my dear..."

"I been a habitue of your preaching since you come to this church, admired your ways and your doings, and how you've been pulling this congregation up, our first Black pastor and all."

"It is my calling."

"But now I see you for true, Preacher. That you got a line drawn you won't cross. Some people just not people to you, is that right?"

"That's not what I meant. It's behavior I'm talking about."

"Behavior? You judge a man on what he do, but don't the scripture say it is not for us to judge? I see what you're up to. You think you can catch me here at home, up to my elbows in laundry on a Friday afternoon, and tell me what to do with my man? Who you think you are Preacher?"

"Martha, now hold yourself. I will not be addressed this way."

"You will not be addressed at all is what I say. Now get on about your business, I got washing to do."

Chapter 32

Egyptian Building Basement

Sometimes a patient from the infirmary upstairs would summon a last ragged burst of energy and make a break for it, turning down the wrong set of stairs to find themselves agog at Baker on his knees on the spattered floor, assembling a skeleton, or up at the lye vat stirring with a paddle in the gloom, the sordid stink of the place staggering, and the snake-like gaze of the little man as he turned to them bowel-loosening. One homeless patient had keeled over on the spot and supplied the dissection table that very day. Others backed away in terror, stumbling into the street's fresh air, where their dying words were of the horrors they'd glimpsed in the college building's basement. They, too, came back to him. In time, so did most of the infirmary patients, quickly from the student doctor surgeries or gradually from whatever diseases wracked them.

He had tied the ankles of the corpse together and weighted its arms ahead of the rigor, had fed the embalming hose into its neck and was working at the groin incision when the stranger cleared her throat. He looked up and was startled himself. The woman who stood before him wore a dress of coarse burlap that fell to ankles adorned with bracelets made of shells, shell necklaces hung to her waist, and she held a tall wooden cane with a vine wrapped about it like a snake. She wore a towering straw hat that rose to a funnel, and her gaze met Baker's with a cold appraisal. This was no infirmary patient.

"What you doin' here, woman?" he demanded.

She came forward, her eyes steady on his face, and the strangest thing, took a deep breath of the stench, allowing herself a satisfied smile as she exhaled. Baker set his scalpel on the corpse's belly and stepped back.

"What you want here, you hear me?," he warned.

The woman turned to gaze about the cellar, with its bunkbed racks, its wood stove, dumping pit, and walls hung with saws and knives. She raised her arms and slowly waved them, like a cormorant down on the river drying its wings, her throat emitting a weird keening sound, a ululating hum that grew louder as she turned, the room's shadows retreating. Then, as if she'd realized how odd this must seem, she dropped her arms and turned back to Baker. She clasped her hands at her breast and sighed, "You could be him, y'all cut from the same mold."

It had been so long and they'd undergone such changes, but now she came to his side and her hand touched his cheek. That's when he fell to his knees, quaking. He wrapped his arms about her legs, sank his face into the course weave of her gown, and sobbed. She stood still, one hand palming his bald skull, the other fingering the scalpel he'd left on the corpse. She was home again, after such ordeals. She had work to do.

CHAPTER 33

HIS MOTHER'S TRIALS

"You Igbo, you know that? You know what that is?"

"Mama, it's late, come now get some supper. What you doin' out here with my lye pot?"

She had walked away before he could stop her, no telling to where, and here she was again a week later, same fantastic costume, right outside the college in the side yard, acting like she owned the place.

"Hush boy. I can help you," she said. "But you got to help me, too. Your daddy and me, we had a deal deeper than some old slave marriage, you know that? You seen his panther bone? That ain't no panther. That a leopard toe from the homeland is what. You even know what a leopard is? You still got it? I hope you buried it with him. He need it on the other side.

"He ever tell you 'bout me? What you 'member from before? But here you stand, bald as a cue ball like the day you come out me. Haints pull your hair out at night, you find it on the pillow in the mornin', am I right? Here look at this."

He'd smelled the rich and smokey aroma of pork fat boiling as he came down the stairs, now stood with the old crone at the fire she'd built practically right out on the street.

With his wooden paddle, she leaned in to stir the vat with a practiced rhythm. Her face blurred in the steam and the salty smell had him swooning. "You workin' cracklin's in there?" he asked.

"A kind a that, bake up a pone, you eat one bite a day til it's gone."

"That's what I'm talkin' 'bout."

"It turn your stomach, good as it taste, but you eat it, hear me?"

"What it do?" He found himself talking like his mother, to his surprise.

"Yo' little heebie-jeebies? Won't help with that. We all got 'em in this line of work, but most folks too dumb to know it."

"Heebie-jeebies, what you know about that?"

"Son. Boy. Some nights I shake my head at all you up to. You know he there, catch him out the corner of yo' eye, you hear that dirty ol' laugh. You his now, don't you know that? Any fool mess with a grave. Yo' daddy, they was a team, made the debbil hisself hold his hat."

She wasn't right, poor woman. Talking out of her head. He had to ask, "What happened to you, Mama?"

"You know it. Sold down the James on Christmas Eve."

"To where? I mean...."

"I tell you one time, we leave it there." She bent to her stirring, salty steam rising around them. He waited, hat in hand.

"You hear tell of a fancy girl? You know what they is? You hear tell a the Mississippi River? Make your little James through here look like a creek. Riverboat, the String of Pearls, they call it. String of pink dicks is what it was. Dress up in petticoats so they can tear 'em off you. Wadn't the worst way, I guess, but some lowdown motherfuckers, too."

"Mama."

"Don't you blubber, boy. Not a day go by I ain't with you all these years. Old man Billie, he knew it. Day he die, I caught a fever, almost went down myself."

"Did what?"

"Stir this pot, boy."

She handed over the ladle and squatted in the building's shade, away from the rising steam. Her face glistened, round, full, somehow yet young, but her eyes black stars that stared right through you.

She said, "One thing to know. Every dick that fucked me fell off. Took a while, no need to rush it, but I know. And that boat the Pearl? Union gunboat took her down Day One of the war, all aboard lost." She snapped her fingers and allowed herself a grim smile.

"How'd you get out?"

"Won't aboard, not me nor the other fancy girls. I seen it all comin', stick a hairpin in the neck of a watchman right where your daddy show me, took a skiff and we drift on by the gunboats, wavin' at the boys in blue, steamin' upriver on their way."

"How did you know it?"

"Stop your stirrin' a minute, boy. Come sit here. Let them cracklin's float."

"What is it?"

"What you think, son? Them haints tell me whatever I care to know."

"You talk to them?"

"You ain't? That the funny part. What you 'fraid of? Boy, you done half crossed over, and the trick now is to hold you back a spell. Yo' daddy never tol' you? You messin' with the deep haints from the old land. Death walker. You even know what that is? And you think you just messin' with bones. You hear what I say?"

"I want some of them cracklin's, you hear what I say?"

She cackled from deep in her throat the way a hen does, then stood and walked back over to the pot, her ebony skin taking on a glistening sheen from the steam rising around them, bare toes like fingers gripping the dry earth. She dug in the vat and lifted the paddle towards him, greasy nobs of pork fat on it dripping. "People after your hide on this side, haints after you on the other. What you need is protection. Take these cracklin's now, bake up a good pone, and keep it to yo'self. Eat a piece a day like I tell you. And when you done, then we see where we at. Say nary a word, not even to yo' Martha, you hear me? Powerful juju in that pone. You eat it all up, then see how it go. See if she don't come back."

CHAPTER 34

HOW IT WENT FOR MARTHA

FOR DAYS no one spoke to her, or even nodded. Side-by-side in the workrooms of the hospital and alms house, taking turns at the washing, then the wringing, and the hauling of heavy baskets out to dry on the line, retrieving the dried linens for pressing and folding, then delivering them upstairs for distribution to the floors, even though each task involved at least two workers, even though their elbows touched and their hands danced alike in the flow, no one acknowledged her as more than those hands. No one sang, no one joked, no one even complained at the heat of a summer come early.

Of course, they'd known who her husband was, so this sudden shunning seemed confounding to Martha. Maybe it was just embarrassment for her, or worse, some kind of delayed pity that she'd taken up with that demon, and even made a child with him. Maybe having it thrown up in their faces at church had brought their judgment to the fore. Or maybe it was the recent article in *The Planet* newspaper, no doubt timed to follow Baptism Sunday's uproar, describing an investigation at the new Oakwood cemetery that had turned up a dozen empty graves, not in the pauper's field, either, but in the private sections advertised as safe from the snatchers. Like Martha, some of her co-workers had studied with Maggie Walker, took pride in reading the paper and sharing its news with their illiterate friends. Some believed it was their own kin torn out of their coffins. She over-heard stage-whispered talk that the men were out to get him for real this time.

Dr. Watkins had read the paper, too. Standing with a crutch a little lopsided on his wooden leg, he was waiting at the barn one afternoon when she returned from work and urged her to warn her husband away for a time. "There is talk of a mob, Martha. The college is a fortress and with the police precinct just down the street, he is safe there. If they find him here, however, I fear for your safety, and my own."

She thanked him and turned on her heel, rushing to school to retrieve her son. Any normal day, he would have found his way home alone, but the older children could be brutal, she knew. She almost missed him in her hurry, but he called to her from the alley where he crouched in tears, his shirt torn and his lip bloodied. All the way home, she shielded him with her shawl from the scowls of neighbors. They made it back to the loft safely, but as they climbed the stairs, she thought that even the old horse in his stall seemed restless and on edge.

All night she fretted, the boy sleeping at her side, and a fire poker – her only weapon – to hand. Surely, he knew the danger. This had always been his concern, but she hadn't really under-stood, had humored him in his surreptitious comings and goings, had made an awful mistake in drawing him out, bringing him into company, pushing him against his will into the daylight affairs of the community. This was all on her, she saw it now. If he came, if he dared the night streets, if he could bring himself to show his face to her after what she'd witnessed in that base-ment slaughterhouse, what would she say to him? How could they go on?

She startled at a sound in the kitchen, something shuffling there. Left the boy and crept to the door, holding the poker in both hands. Moonlight at the window made the room an ink sketch. No place there to hide. But then a flutter at her head; she swung the poker, striking nothing. And then she saw it, a bird of some kind, or maybe a bat, had got in through the open window. She swung the poker again, just missed, and saw the shadowy creature sail like a kite back out into the sky and disappear. She slammed the window and fell heavily into her chair. Was she awake? Was this a bad dream? The heavy poker in her hand was real, that was for sure.

And then it came to her, of course, this is what we must do. That night bird, whatever it was, had shown the way. They were all in danger now. Somehow she had to get to Chris. Like that bird, they had to go.

CHAPTER 35

REVEREND BARRET'S PARSONAGE - COLUMBIA, VIRGINIA

"KIND OF YOUR COUSIN TAKIN' us in like this."

Martha grasped her husband's hand and guided him down a tree-lined lane towards the river.

"You ever been to the country before?" she asked.

"Not like this, no. Out by Oakwood graveyard, still some trees."

"You like it?"

Baker swatted at a bee circling his head. "Take some gettin' used to," he smiled.

"You smilin', though, that's good."

"I feared you was gone."

"Just walk with me now, I'm here."

"If they'd killed me dead, way I was without you...."

"Don't talk like that, Chris." She stopped him and met his gaze. "You know, a laundry woman sees a lot. Windin' sheets, blood and maggots all in 'em, birthin' sheets, too. Smeared with that consumption snot, the stinky sweat from fevers, all torn up from who knows what."

"But you never saw that."

"No. And I never hope to again."

"You won't. You stay away from that place."

"We're far away from all that. Just walk with me in all the pretty. Nobody's comin' out this way for you. Nobody knows you're here."

"Word travel."

"Hush, now, take a seat, husband."

It was the first time since she'd come for him that she'd used that word. He'd been out back of the college, cooking something in a pot, but she had train tickets in her hand, and only needed to say four words, "We got to go."

Nobody to stop him. School out, all the professors off on their travels. And there she stood, and if she'd told him to stand on his head and spin, he'd have tried.

They sat together on the trunk of a downed tree at the river's edge and considered their situation. Martha's cousin the Reverend James Barrett owned acreage along the river, where he'd planted tobacco and some corn. A cow wandered daisy-dotted pasture on the lowland. Same river as Richmond, that dirty city downstream fifty miles, and what a difference in that distance!

Baker said, "Everything here smell so sweet. I mean, the trees got a sweet smell, and the grass, hay in the barn. And the river up here ain't like she is down Richmond way, got a froggy smell make you want to jump right in."

They had caught a night train up the river, Baker faking a cough behind a bandanna in the colored car, his wife fanning him as if he had a fever, praying all the while he'd go unrecognized. They'd gotten off at Point of Fork depot before dawn and walked to the farm through the sleepy town, where no one she hoped had a clue what janitoring at a Medical College entailed.

It wasn't a topic either cared to re-visit, and for the rest of their lives neither would go there, but just this once Martha dared it. She covered her husband's hand with both of hers and asked, "What happened at the church, Chris? What was it?"

Tears welled in his eyes and his lips trembled as he searched for some word. At last he said, "My mama come back, you know that?"

"Your mother? What? You never said."

"No," he sighed, tears at his cheeks, "just of recent, since all them doin's."

"Where is she?" Martha asked.

"Down Richmond way still, I figure. She come and go, won't say where."

"Oh my, we left her behind."

"She been through a lot. Don't seem right, neither."

"Your mother. After all these years. Can we send a message, ask someone to go find her?"

"Where to look? 'Fraid to leave a note when we took off, somebody else see it and catch us here."

"Oh but Chris, your mother! We'll find a way. Yes we will." She ran her thumb down his cheek to wipe at a tear.

They watched the water running at their feet, river always moving, always in one place. On the opposite bank a trio of children waded in, laughing and gabbing. Their son Johnny among them. "He's gettin' used to it pretty fast, city boy that he is," Martha smiled.

"They think he know everything, all schooled up, seen the world."

"First time he's ever gone barefoot outside, tippin' along like a white girl."

"He far from that."

The children splashed out into the current, up to their waists, teasing each other to go further. Johnny waved at his parents and led the way across the stream. He looked back at the two girls, and then shouted. One of them was gone.

Martha had thrown off her shoes and jumped in the river before Baker could stir from his revery. He watched her churning in slow motion against the weight of the moving water, her knees kicking high. Johnny squatted, letting the current float him downstream. The remaining girl stood in knee deep water, wailing. Baker threw off his shoes and stepped into sucking mud at the riverbank. He should go in, he knew. Martha and Johnny had disappeared around a swift running bend. He yelled for the girl to stay put and steeled himself to go to her, but he too stood frozen in place.

"Chris, come down here, you gotta come!" he heard Martha yell. He could see her on a sand bank a hundred yards downstream, waving wildly. Johnny stood at her side, and at her feet lay the girl who'd gone under.

"Come now, girl," Chris beckoned. "Come on over here now, find a rock to step on."

The girl knew the river well, had led the trio across before, and she was at his side in an instant.

"She musta hit that catfish hole! I told her stay with me!" she cried.

Chris took off down the river bank, fighting brush all the way. When he got to the sand bar, Martha was crouched next to the girl, sobbing.

"She gone, Daddy, she gone," Johnny said.

Indeed the girl lay limp as a doll, her dress soaked and her bare legs dripping. Reverend Barrett's baby she was, too.

What happened next he would never tell, not even to Martha. The heckling voice that haunted his every hour spoke clearly, five words, right into his head, "You know what to do."

And he did, too. It was not something he'd ever seen anyone attempt before, but it made sense. What was killing her was them lungs behind her ribs, soggy with river water. He had to pump them up again, get them blowing, so he bent to the girl's lips, squeezed her nose tight, and puffed into her mouth as hard as he could. His mind's eye saw it all, the rubbery airway in her throat splitting off at her breast bone, its branches running down to those paired pink balloons heavy with water. He caught his breath a second and was at it again, puff and gasp, puff and gasp.

"What you doin' Daddy?" the boy asked, aghast at his father's weird kiss.

But then the girl sputtered. Water dribbled from her mouth. Baker lifted her head, turned her and swatted her back, hoping to push more water out of her sodden lungs. She coughed, then sat up on her own, and looked around in surprise. Martha and Johnny stood stunned. The older girl was already off running back to the house, with a wondrous story to tell.

IT HAPPENED AGAIN, a week later, when Martha borrowed a buggy to visit her cousin Dorothy in Cloverdale several miles upstream. They found the old woman laid out on a pallet by the cabin door, too weak to sit up, her daughter fanning her.

"Doctor come by this mornin', bled her pretty good. She weak as a noodle now," the woman explained.

"How long she been down like this?" Baker asked.

"Took to bed in March, cain't seem to get goin'. We 'fraid it's consumption and we all catch it, too."

"That ain't it," Baker said. "I seen a lot a that, this somethin' else."

"Oh you a doctor, is you?" the woman frowned.

"'Bout the furtherest thing from that," he said, "but look here, don't let them doctors bleed her no more. They dryin' her out. She need that blood to run around inside, keep her juicy."

"What do you know about all that, Chris?" Martha asked.

"I don't know what I know, woman, and that's the truth, but y'all stop cuttin' on this old lady. And 'nother thing, sit her up pat on her back like a drum long as she can take it. Like this here."

Martha raised her hand at her cousin's protest, a little surprised herself at her husband's command, then bent to help him tip the old woman upright. He sat behind her on the floor, leaned her forward and thumped on her back with both hands. "Like that, see? You try that, too, when you can."

"And another thing, get a fresh cow bone or two, cook you up some marrow broth, and you spoon that down her throat. That marrow's where the blood come from."

A week later, when they returned, the old lady was sitting in a cane rocker on the cabin stoop, contentedly humming. In two weeks she was back in her garden, and her daughter out spreading the miracle all over Fluvanna County, about this little man make a potion lift Mama from death's door, ain't no doctor with his razor come 'round here no more. Before the month was out, that story, and the previous miracle, which Reverend Barrett had praised with sobs on his knees from the pulpit – the resurrection of his dear daughter by the kiss of this stranger – brought a row of wagons to the parsonage, with ailing elders and wounded workers laid out in back.

Baker greeted them all, tried to make sense of their ailments, and treated them like machines made out of meat. Some needed a little spritz of oil, others something to prime the tap, some a dip in cold water to cool 'em down. In almost every case, his patients said what he recommended was exactly the opposite of what the doctor had prescribed. And their payment for his labors, nearly always a live chicken or guinea hen, soon filled the parson's coop, so he and Baker had to build another next to it.

Sitting on the porch stoop, admiring their work, the little

shed with its pine board siding slatted for ventilation, its neatly laid cedar shake roof, and the laddered ramp that led up to a chicken-sized door with a fox-proof latch, the preacher said, "They's somethin' 'bout you, Chris. Look at all you done for our folks 'round here. I believe you got the shine son. The Lord of Light has laid his Hand on you."

Baker watched the band of hens pacing the yard, rhythmically pecking as they went, no thought of any other heaven in their tiny heads. He almost said it, but let it slide, "Somethin' may got a hold of me, alright, but it ain't no Lord of Light." The preacher didn't seem to notice the hulking shadow in the wrong place, on the sunny side of the coop, and if he heard that hearty guffaw, probably chalked it up to an owl.

CHAPTER 36

A VISITOR FROM THE CITY

THEY'D BEEN at Reverend Barret's house all Summer, sharing the upstairs loft, when a familiar carriage appeared in the yard. Tall white man with sky blue eyes that shone a mile off. The young Dr. Stuart McGuire himself, son of the old war veteran Hunter. Had driven that rig fifty miles, sleeping over at a tavern in Goochland along the way. Dr. McGuire unfolded himself from the driver's seat, hopped down smartly, and nodded as the minister's daughter took the horse's reins. He pulled a handkerchief from his pocket to wipe his brow, then gazed about at the tidy farm and parsonage.

"Young woman," he said, "I seek the renowned healer of Fluvanna County, fellow named Chris Baker. You know of him?"

"I do, suh. Seen that man raise up my little sister from dead out cold."

"You don't say?"

"Doctor McGuire," Baker called, easing open the cottage's screen door. "You come all this way?"

"A pleasant drive along the river for the most part, and for one reason only. I'm here for you, Chris. We need you at our new institute. Term starts in two weeks."

Baker stepped onto the porch, tin water bucket in hand. "You know what happen I go back there."

"We need you. Both the Medical College and our new school, as well. No one can do this work as you do."

"Don't know 'bout that."

Doctor McGuire strode to the porch step, and took the offered drink from a dipper. He asked, "What is this I hear of you practicing some kind of medical specialty hereabouts?"

"Ain't all that. Just figurin' from what I learnt about bones and whatnot."

"Figuring? Hmm. I always say, not a doctor in the South knows more about human anatomy than Chris Baker."

"May be right about that."

"Well, I believe so. Which is why I've come here these two days on my errand. To recruit you. We can hire a janitor, but we need your unique talents. Will double your pay at the start of term, increase your remittance for anatomy material by one dollar per item, and you may continue at the Medical College as before. "

"Kind of you to go all that," Baker smiled. Then he leaned to the doctor's ear and whispered, "But they see me, they still gon' kill me."

"Who will kill you, Chris?"

"Ain't a colored man in Richmond ain't after my neck is who."

"You will be safe in our care."

"Long as I hide in the basement, yeah. Stick my head out in daylight, get it shot clean off."

"They will learn that you are here, Chris. They will come for you."

"Who tell 'em that, now?"

"Batteaux boats and trains up and down this river every day, Chris. You will be safer with us."

"You come all this way, did you?"

"I shall overnight at Dr. Snead's in Fork Union. Discuss this with your dear wife and son. She would no longer need to run laundry, you know, unless of course, she cares to."

"You said enough already."

"Well, consider my offer, Chris. At our new institute, just around the corner from the Medical College, we shall do things right. Scientifically. We anticipate at least as many students on opening as the Medical College enrolls in any year. You may stay on there, as before, but serve our needs as well, as I'm sure you can manage."

"Suh." Baker gazed down the shaded lane to the river landing in the distance and took a lung-filling breath of the fragrant farmyard breeze.

"I shall return tomorrow for your reply," McGuire said, turning back to his carriage. "Did you see what they called you in the city paper last month? 'Doctor Baker.' If we are to credit the tales heard on my journey out this way, folks hereabouts would concur."

CHAPTER 37

BRUSH ARBOR

"How you find us here, Mama? Why you hide out in these buggy old woods? Preacher got room. You take the loft with Angel, the boy and me can sack out in the barn."

She'd made a camp in a grove of poplars, and squatted there now before a guttering fire, stirring a stewpot set on glowing coals, and dressed in that old burlap shift she'd worn on the day of her return. Barefoot, her long toes clutching the earth the way a bird sits a tree branch, her silvered hair matted into long ropes that dangled like snakes about her face.

"Naw, son. Had 'nuff a walls 'round me. Brush arbor when it rain, back where Old Man Barrett used to preach 'fore they built the church-house. Look here, got all we need right here, see what these woods give up this mornin'?"

Baker kneeled at her side as she unrolled a kerchief on the ground, then sorted the pile of twigs and roots it held. "This one here, look like a man, that the real conjure root, been seekin' him out a long time. Little sliver of him, make a ol' grandpa buck like a stallion. Get a pretty penny for that root down in Richmond, you talk to them ol' witchers in the Slip. These here pointy leaves, you dry 'em up, make a tea, shit a body out good, they need that. This one, call it James Town weed, got a kindly and a ornery side to it, like most things. You havin' restless sleep or a guilty mind, make a tea a this, you go right out like a baby. But watch you don't sip it that eighth day in a row, then you ain't wake up. In the old days, a woman put that in they ol' master's tea. Shoot, any of these greens, you get some, go good with them bones you got. Conjure man clear out to Memphis, down Vicksburg way, pay real money, you make up a trick bag."

"You find all these weeds out here by the river?"

"A treasure here, boy. Frogs and dragonflies. Copperhead snakes. Powerful roots up in these woods, son. Nothin' like it in the city."

"You got somethin' help the Preacher's mama?"

"She got the stroke, is it? Dead all down one side?"

"Woke up last week couldn't get out of bed."

She stood up and allowed her back a stretch, then pulled a sturdy hickory stick out of her kindling pile. "Alright," she said, "take this here stick, soak it good in some mule piss for three days, so it swell up. Peel off the bark and grind that up in the Preacher's corn mill he use for his chicken feed. Keep the stick, too. Here, take it now."

"What will that do?"

"It the debbils. We got to call 'em outta her. Mix that bark meal with some mustard seed, some jimsom, old girl's daughter got to rub her hard on that whole dead side from the tip of her finger to the tip of her toe, don't miss a spot neither. Every mornin' when the rooster crow she start."

"You best come do this. They ain't listen to me."

"You do as I say, they listen. Now this what you do. You hold that stick over her, say what you want, the words will come, and if they don't make sense, even better. Just hold still. Tell her kick that stick with her bad foot, tell her grab that stick with that old dead hand a hers. Tell her she can do it, she just try. Don't let her kick with the good foot nor reach with the good hand. Get her daughter hold her down, if you need to. You do that every day once the daughter rub her good, or if you cain't get there, teach the Preacher, keep at it long as the old lady can take it."

"What will that do?"

"That mule piss. Draw the debbil outta her, the death layin' on her soul, it go up in the stick, that old piss get the debbil drunk, and now he stuck up in there, cain't get out. Day she grab that stick you done. Bring it to me. Stick with a debbil in it make a powerful charm. Make a good walkin' cane, too."

"Come up to the house, will you?"

"Brush arbor do for me, boy, you get on."

"I won't quit askin'."

"No you won't, but I say back the same." She held out the hickory stick in both hands, palms up, as if handing him a sword. When he took it he startled, a buzz running up his arm like the stick was full of bees. She allowed a thin-lipped grin, before turning back to her fire.

"Mama, Dr. McGuire come up here, all the way from the city."

"Seen it."

"Wants me back, got a new college startin', say he needs what I do real bad."

"Make him pay you, boy."

"Says he will. It's them bullets, though."

"Them bullets find you here 'fore long." She crouched down with a twig and stirred ashes at the fire's edge, tracing some kind of figure there. "Tell you what. Come back here in four days, be a full moon, I have somethin' for you."

"'Nother fox foot?"

"Somethin' like that. You keep that one, too."

"Come home, Mama."

"Boy, you go look after your own."

"You my own, too."

"No, you mine. That ain't the same. Take that stick, do what I say. See if that old girl don't get up off her bed. And save that debbil stick for me when she back up and around, too. Be a treasure, you know how to use it."

CHAPTER 38

THE COLLEGE OF PHYSICIANS AND SURGEONS, RICHMOND

"WE HAVE great expectations for our partnership, here, Chris," said Dr. McGuire. "Allow me to show you the anatomy works, which I do hope will be to your liking."

Baker pulled up his coat collar, stepped hesitantly out of the carriage, and slipped inside the imposing Clay Street edifice as quickly as he could. He'd insisted on meeting at night, and old man McGuire had sent a covered jitney to Dr. Watkins' home, driven by a medical student, at midnight. The new building fronted half a street block and loomed four stories high, but to Baker's relief, it looked like an office building, not weird like the medical school. Once inside, the doctor wasted no time in launching into his tour.

"We are entering a new age of medicine, as I'm sure you are aware," he smiled. "Note the electric bulbs that light our rooms. And now, you must have heard, the Anatomical Act has taken effect, granting our medical schools the bodies of prison inmates and alms house residents otherwise unclaimed. Which we hope will mean that your efforts in our cemeteries may be ended."

"How many stiffs you need this year?" Baker asked.

"We intend to provide a first rate, scientific, and rigorous education, and our initial class will top one hundred students, which I daresay is more than your current and my former institution has on its roll. My thought would be fifty cadavers, thereabouts, this coming term."

"And that number again for the Medical College. You think we can get that many out of the jails and the poor house?"

"Do you think otherwise?"

"Well, law or not, been haulin' stiffs outta both them places all these years, and still need to dig, and that before you got to workin' on this new school."

"Yes, well, as that may be, allow me to demonstrate these other features of our facility that may allay your concerns."

Dr. McGuire led Baker to a humming tin box, nearly as tall as he was, with a metal door on one side. "This machine here, rather straightforward to operate, we imported from Germany, and I believe it may be the first of its type on this side of the Atlantic. Open the door and step inside, if you will."

Baker hesitated, but pulled a latch on the shiny door, then stepped back in surprise as a wave of cold air struck his face. Dr. McGuire crouched down to step inside, and explained, "Shelves here, when built, will hold six adult cadavers at a steady temperature near freezing."

"Ice box," Baker mused.

"Not ice, chemicals that react to cool the room, ammonia among them. Ice would melt, but this box, we call it a refrigerator, will stay cool, without ice at all, even during our summers."

McGuire closed the metal door and led Baker to another room where gleaming cauldrons as large as the refrigerator lined the wall. "These, Chris, are our formaldehyde tanks, which will provide a much sturdier way of preserving tissue than salt. Once embalmed, using your usual procedure, we shall simply pickle cadavers in these vats, and remove them as needed. Bodies preserved in this way can last a year or more, though our students will have put an end to them well before that."

"This mighty fine, doctor, but if stiffs will keep in your refrigerator and your vats, you still thinkin' you need fifty a year?"

"That is your bailiwick, Chris. We shall see how the term progresses. But my sincere hope is that your future work will entirely involve maintaining legally acquired materials, no more cemetery jaunts for you."

"And Dean Tompkins at the college say he alright with me workin' both sides of the track like this?"

"My former colleagues at the College and I disagree, and I daresay we shall compete, over a great many things, Chris, but on one point we concur. There is no man in the Commonwealth who can do so well what you do, and if you agree to parse your labors between us, then Dr. Tompkins and I shall happily accept that arrangement."

"I keep my old room in the basement?"

"Your choice, of course, as your main employ will continue as before, but to demonstrate our commitment to your efforts, allow me to show you the special accommodation that Dr. Tompkins and I are constructing, at no small cost, entirely for your safety and protection. Open this door here."

An oaken door in the wall opened, like that of the refrigerator, to a cool draft. "You make a cave in here?" Baker asked.

"We are linking to a tunnel laid directly through the garden of the old Confederate White House, from your basement lodgings to our laboratory here. Once completed, you will be able to pass between our institutions in complete security underground!"

Baker stood for a long minute at the threshold, staring into the dark passage. Finally, he said, "Well, doctor, I been a groundhog all these years, poppin' up outta my hole. Y'all do this, reckon y'all made a full-time mole outta me now."

Dr. McGuire, taking that as a quip, replied with a wry smile, "Welcome back, Chris. Welcome home."

The Interview

"If we might go back for a moment, you mentioned your father?"

Baker nodded, *"Daddy raised me up in this work; he gone."*

"Mother?"

Baker nodded, let his gaze fall past the reporter's shoulder for a thoughtful moment, then busied himself refilling his pipe.

"People have said you have a wife?"

He lifted the pipe to his lips, lit it while drawing slow puffs, then settled into his smoke as if he hadn't heard the question.

"Chris?" the reporter chided.

"This ain't about family, this about me, is what you said."

"It's a yes or no question."

"No it ain't."

"Do you fear for their protection?"

"Would you?"

"Then I take that as a yes."

"You can take it out the door right now, you makin' all this up anyway."

"A child?"

"We 'bout done here, you keep at it." Baker pushed himself up from the chair and turned towards the stairs.

"No, forgive me," the reporter pleaded, *"Let me return to my notes, to your work. This key question, I must ask before we're done, how many graves would you say, across your long career, have you emptied of their contents?"*

Baker paused, and spoke over his shoulder, *"Ain't take nothin' but the stiffs. What else in there, leave that to the grave."*

"Of course, understood. But how many bodies would you say?"

He turned around to face the reporter again, a half-smile at his lips. *"Oh now, ain't never toted that up."*

Chapter 39

Egyptian Building - 1893

The basement door thudded like somebody was kicking it, maybe the staver with new barrels, but Baker slipped an ice pick in his apron pocket anyway. When he pulled the door open, the man at the threshold stood panting, his face haggard and his eyes a rheumy red. He was not, however, wearing his usual policeman's double-breasted coat with brass buttons, but a shabby tab jacket and patched pants.

"Officer Searcy," Baker nodded, "Been a while."

"Ain't no officer, no more," the man growled. "All your doin's, too!"

Searcy stepped closer, reeking of whiskey. He peered past Baker into the basement gloom, growling, "Ol' Chris hisself, the hospital janitor. Body snatchin' goblin is what you are."

"What you need, Searcy? What you here for?"

The man fumbled in his jacket, maybe searching for a bottle, and warmed to his rant. "I know what you are, Baker. You ain't just some hospital cleanup man, you ain't just some grave-robbin' darkey. You the Mayor of N___town, is what. I seen it. You got half the city on your books – smithies, train conductors, stevedores – all of 'em in your pay."

"Get on, son, go home now," Baker chided, one hand on the door, the other grasping the ice pick in his pocket.

"And your woman's in it, too, makin' her rounds at the poor house, asylum, even the city jail, that busy bitch, with her laundry outfit, nice how she keeps an eye out for any poor soul about to drop, so you know exactly where and when to haul up with your butcher wagon! Yeah, you got one sweet deal goin' here, you Baker's, you do that!"

This was dangerous talk, bringing Angel into it, but drunk as he was, Searcy didn't seem to know that or care. At last he found what he was searching for, not a bottle, but a dun colored pistol, palm-sized, like a lady might carry in her purse. Baker watched him fumble with it, as if he didn't know which end was the barrel, but he soon figured it out, and pointed the gun directly at Baker's chest.

"Well, Chris, here we go. Let's see what your old hoodoo magic does for you today. You got past me last time, boy, but now you're mine."

"I done nothin' to harm you, Searcy. You just drunk. Get on away from here now."

"I know what you did, Chris. They shoulda strung you up them times we caught you in the graveyard. My own baby daughter Cissy turned yellow and coughed herself to death in my arms. Wife gone off her head now. I know one thing, sober or not, that it all comes back to you Chris Baker. Now die, won't you, and see who chops up your black ass!"

Baker sat down hard with the bullet's impact. It passed through his wool coat, imbedded itself in the rubber apron, and cracked a rib near his sternum, he figured right above his heart. The hot slug fell into his hand. He looked up at his incredulous assailant, offering the bullet held up in his palm. Calmly, without surprise or rancor, he said, "Searcy, you need work. I could use a diggin' man."

"Oh dear Lord, what are you Chris Baker? What are you, after all?" the man cried. He shoved the little pistol back into his pocket and backed away, stumbling down the hill on the cobblestones. Baker climbed to his feet, closed and locked the door. He dropped the spent bullet in his pocket alongside the ice pick, then felt inside his shirt for the welt forming there. Thick rubber apron with the leather backing did good. He eased down in the old rocking chair and lit his pipe, then shook his head, "What you done, Mama? What hex you put on that poor man and his people?"

HE FOUND her at her work bench in the stable, bundling dried frogs in red flannel tied with ribbon. "Why you out in the daytime, boy?" she asked.

Baker set a sack of dried ears on the table. "Searcy boy, police that put me in jail. You workin' him?"

"Don't mess with white folk, you know that, son."

"Them men, you said you fixed 'em pretty good, messed with you on that boat."

"A long time back that was. Colored folk keep me busy hereabouts."

"But you do know this Searcy man?"

"Ain't nothin' but a sprinkle powder, spread at his gate, one time is all. Ain't meant to do all that."

"You even know what that stuff can do, old woman?"

"It you, son, it ain't me. You got a parade a haints trailin' you, at yo' beck and call. You be careful who you waggle yo' finger at. No tellin' what they might do."

"Haints done it, is that your play?"

"I ain't touch that man's baby nor his wife neither. This on you, son. Ain't you seen what all this' diggin' has riz up?"

"I seen 'em, yes I have. Ain't but some bad dreams."

"I see 'em right now. You want me axe 'em they names?"

"Mama," he cautioned.

"I ain't touch that baby."

Baker shook his head. "Here. You got any use for a bullet fired in anger?"

"Shit, throw it in the bucket with them from the war. That Searcy boy pop you?"

"Right here." He bared his shirt to show her the lump.

"Bullet bounce off you now, do it? See what I say? Now you wait, that story get out, some crazy doin's 'round here 'fore long. You best stay in yo' hole." She handed him one of the tied bundles, adding, "Put this pouch on your bump."

"Come to my place, Mama. You still ain't met my Angel and my boy all this time."

"I seen 'em, mighty nice folks."

"You met her? She never said."

"I ain't said we met, said I seen her."

"Well, come, then, come stay with them, we got room."

"I got my own place is fine, son. Don't you fret 'bout me."

"But why won't you come, then, share a meal with us?"

"You hardly get over there yo'self. That's yo' time, ain't mess with that."

"They'd love to meet you, Mama."

"Well, in good time, but this ain't it, so leave it there."

"What will you do?"

"Naw, that the question you need to be axing yo'self. Preacher say they's a shine on you, boy. What you gon' do 'bout that?"

CHAPTER 40

PROFESSOR TAYLOR'S LECTURE - 1894

THE FALL OPERA season had just begun, traveling companies from the north arriving by train each week, but no one, it seemed, could resist the lure of this lecture. Professor Taylor himself, that raconteur and rascal, both chief chemist at the Medical College and the city's coroner, planned to address the item topmost on the minds of everyone from scullery maid to governor in the city, would they but admit it: ghosts. Since the war, sightings had seemed to multiply each year. Slamming doors, phantom hands at the throat or up a lady's petticoat, the moaning and dragging of chains, invisible troops marching on the cobblestones, gossamer figures on the stairs. Was there anyone who had not experienced some kind of haunting? Even the newspapers had taken up the call, reporting on the latest dramatic event, some priest's effort at exorcism or a hoodoo's dance across the river.

People sniffed, laughed it off, called it superstition or nervous exhaustion, until they themselves began to suspect a flicker or shadow at the corner of an eye, a window shutter flying up, or the way a rain spout seemed to speak in muttered voices. And the good professor's choice of venue could not have been more inspired, the auditorium of the Medical College. If any building anywhere could rival a cemetery in its invocation of the supernatural, this was it. Few had previously dared or had reason to climb the steps of the imposing edifice, crossing between its shadowed columns into its high-ceilinged vestibule, to stand arrested at the sounds and scents of death and dying wafting therein. The floor directly above the auditorium housed the infirmary, where any ailing patient able to do so leaned out a window, gasping for breath. Beneath the floorboards lurked the notorious basement, where rumored horrors abounded. The auditorium itself, however, was as grand as any theater on Broad Street, an arc of cushioned chairs, seating for 700, on a downward tilt towards the stage. The four corners of the room featured magnificent arrangements of the most aromatic flowers, in vases tall as a man, but – was this intended or ineradicable? – an unmistakable odor yet permeated the still air.

Carriages lined up along College Street two hours before curtain time. Students took tickets and hung coats on racks in the vestibule. By 8 o'clock the auditorium was full, the walls crowded with standing attendees. Everyone had come prepared, the ladies with handkerchiefs soaked in cologne, the men with cigars, all those mingled fumes confounding the stench, but no one dared to leave their seat, the audience tittering, as if expecting an announcement of war.

A gasp as a student flipped a switch to dim the new electric lights, a spot shone onto the podium, and there he stood, the rascal himself, Professor Taylor in evening dress, his thick bottle glasses enlarging his eyes and making them seem to pulse hypnotically. A tall man, bald up top, his mouth obscured by an unruly white bush of beard and mustache, he stood beaming at what he had accomplished, in one night balancing the college's precarious books, and now prepared to thrill his neighbors, huddled like children about a campfire.

"Welcome, fellow Richmonders, to our Citadel," he announced, long arms sweeping up in greeting. "This Medical College, the only one across the whole Confederacy that stayed open and instructed young surgeons for the battlefield every day of the long war, this infirmary that takes in the least and sickest among us, these clinics where young men learn secrets known only to the medical profession, from whence they go forth to heal, this edifice that yes, has known death and the detailed dissection of the human body, where better in this whole land to examine the phenomenon before us, the topic of my dissertation tonight, and one that appears of keen interest to all gathered here: Is it Superstition? Or is it Real?"

Baker had been unable to find any living soul willing to help him clean the auditorium, so he had done it himself, not just scrubbing the floors and walls, but taking a brush to each of the 700 horsehair seats. He had not slept, but at the Fessor Doctor's keen request, had donned his suit and derby hat, not worn, he thought, for years, and waited as bid, behind a side curtain at the foot of the stage, shaking his head at Taylor's always entertaining folderol, and wondering what part he might be asked to play in this affair.

"I must ask you – each alone in your true heart," Taylor intoned, "Have you seen a ghost?"

Baker peered around the curtain at the crowd. They sat like so many toads, quivering, as if about to leap. But none did. Their silence was to be expected, of course. He might as well have asked them if any were incontinent or impotent or menstruating.

Taylor paused, relishing their quiver and titter, an auditorium overflowing with the city's elite white burghers and their ladies, in the palm of his hand. He answered for them. "Well, look about you, my friends, where other than amidst one of our storied battlefields or cemeteries would you be more likely to encounter an apparition? Our students thrive among the dead, dozens of cadavers each year meet the scalpel in the atrium above your heads. Beneath our feet steams the lye vat that makes a final soup of this material. Look about you, I say. Bring a cot, sometime, you are welcome to stay the night, if you will, and share tea with our famous and devoted custodian and diener, beloved of our students going on two generations now. Come forward, Chris Baker! Take a bow before the audience, will you?"

So this was it. He stepped from behind the curtain, momentarily blinded by the spotlight's sweep, but doffed his hat and bowed deeply to the crowd's applause. Here he stood, the Fessor Doctor's prime example of the terrors he was here to elucidate, the city's own living ghoul on display. Baker turned back to the curtain, but before he could go, Taylor called out, "Ahh, my fellow Virginians, I see that you have some acquaintance with our Mr. Baker, no doubt from his frequent appearances in our newspapers of late. Who among us, I inquire, would have more likely crossed paths with what he so colloquially terms, haints?"

Yes, they all thought, this gnomelike fellow with the unsettling gaze, think what he must have seen and done, unspeakable acts of rapacity in the cemeteries, of butchery within these walls!

"So allow me to inquire, shall we?" Taylor asked.

Necks craned. The professor would have his fiend speak!

"Tell us, Chris, if you will, are you afraid of ghosts?"

Baker allowed a slight smile, pausing, one might think theatrically, before replying. Like the Fessor Doctor, after years with all those students, he too could play an audience. But in truth his pause was not meant to entertain, but only to register the phalanx of ghostly figures fogging the stage. They hung in the cigar smoke, hazy, gimpy and ragged, a whole troupe of the dead. Chris wondered if anyone else in the auditorium could see them, could at least vaguely sense their presence, or hear their shuffle and muffled groans? Surely, these paying attendees had come here tonight out of some awareness, some hint or clue, or longing.

He felt a sharp nudge in the ribs, that impatient river monster, no doubt, so smoothed the front of his coat, and lifted his head with the same air of calm authority the students knew so well, replying, "Afraid of ghosts? No suh. No ghost ain't bother me. It's the livin' I'm askeer'ed of!"

Eruption in the auditorium, cascading laughter, the building tension brilliantly relieved. Professor Taylor beamed. Born showman, that Chris! His breaking out the vernacular always soothes the brows of our people. And he was speaking the truth, too. Some of the ticket money tonight would go to replace windows marred by bullet holes and to install steel doors with oaken crossbeams at the basement entrances.

"There you have it, my friends! From the mouth of our leading authority on all things funereal! Whatever you may have imagined or rumored or suspected, please rest assured, and take it from Ol' Chris himself, 'There ain't no such thang as ghosts!'"

On that point, Baker knew, the Fessor Doctor would digress for an hour or so, making sure to give the people their money's worth in anecdote and homily, though truly, they'd already seen and heard (and smelled) all that they'd come for. But the thing was, he'd asked the wrong question. As he retired behind the curtain, he sniffed the river scent of the beast and heard his clacking skulls, that leering belly mouth teasing, *Can smell the rot on 'em already, eh, Chris? They only here a minute. Be mine in a finger snap.*

Baker grabbed at the curtain to steady himself. He shook his head to clear it, and waved the creature away, his hand passing through its hulking, quavering shape as through a cobweb.

You won't always be so haughty, the river creature smirked.

"Reckon not," Baker replied to the empty stairwell, "but while I breathe, you steer clear. Man's got work to do."

CHAPTER 41

THE MARABLE CASE - 1896

"OH MY, what has Tompkins done now," Dr. McGuire asked, accepting the newspaper offered by his anatomy demonstrator at the door of his Grace Street carriage house.

"Sorry to bother you at home, sir, but it's *The Planet* again, the colored paper. I'm afraid that its editor Mr. Mitchell has embroiled himself deeply in the Marable case."

"I know that already. He and a delegation of Negro ministers came here to request Marable's body, hanged in Lynchburg yesterday, and claimed by law for our uses at the university."

"Yes sir, as detailed in this article, which occupies the front page of his paper this morning. To his credit, Mitchell printed your order releasing the body to his care, and thanks you for permitting him to ship Marable home to his wife in North Carolina, as was the man's dying wish. Did you know that Marable from the scaffold named a white man as the killer?"

"Come in, have a seat, I was just at breakfast. Let me see what our Mr. Mitchell has wrought today." McGuire cinched his dressing gown and beckoned his colleague inside.

The young doctor removed his hat and stepped into the hall-way. "Thank you, sir, I will. You see, it seems that the case does not end there. The body found its way to the Medical College, I'm afraid."

"Dean Tompkins?"

"Nowhere to be found. This appears to be the work of Dr. Matthews, their new anatomist."

"How did he acquire Marable's corpse?"

"The article makes no accusation, but the insinuation, quite strong in its way, is that Matthews commandeered the body for dissection at the college. And went so far as to have Mitchell arrested for trying to recover it for burial!"

"Arrested Mitchell! The editor of the city's chief Black paper? He has swatted the hornet's nest now! Mitchell will have the whole colored populace of this city up in arms! Dear Lord, what has become of that man?"

"Of Matthews, sir?"

"Well yes, him, too, but I mean Marable, where are the man's remains at this time?"

"Well, this is where the Medical College will have work to do. Whereas you and the university are complimented for your gentlemanly compliance with the widow's request and the dying man's last wish, Matthews and the Medical College, your former colleagues, take the brunt of it, as well they might."

"Well, as told by *The Planet*."

"Yes sir, but see this? It's not just Mitchell's opinion this time. The editor got into the college building. Along with the funeral director, Mr. Seldon, who was charged with transporting the body home."

"And?"

"To the dissection theater, sir."

"Oh my. Let me see that paper."

He read:

We present a rough drawing as well as we can recollect it, of the sight that greeted us when, after an hour's work, Chris Baker beckoned us to enter. The body was protruding from a barrel, eyes filled with salt, mouth open, tongue slightly protruding, arms extended, while the salt mixed with blood which had been wasted lay on the floor.

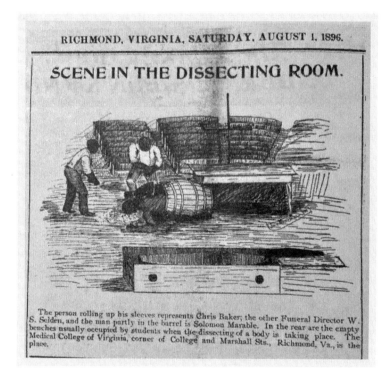

RICHMOND, VIRGINIA, SATURDAY, AUGUST 1, 1896.

SCENE IN THE DISSECTING ROOM.

The person rolling up his sleeves represents Chris Baker; the other Funeral Director W. S. Selden, and the man partly in the barrel is Solomon Marable. In the rear are the empty benches usually occupied by students when the dissecting of a body is taking place. The Medical College of Virginia, corner of College and Marshall Sts., Richmond, Va., is the place.

The empty benches loomed up as shown in the picture, while Chris Baker danced around as unconcerned as though he was in a brick-yard. What cared he? The sight of the horrid-looking corpse or "stiff" as he called it enthused him. The issuing of the gas from the mouth and nostrils of the deceased afforded him amusement. "One more pull, Selden, come on!" Each took hold of one arm they pulled as men would, tugging for dear life. "Can't get it out to-night! I can't get it out to-night! Come in the morning! Say what time you'll be here and it'll be alright. Pull any more, burst the knee-pans off."

Rev. W. F. Graham and Rev. W. R. Gullins were admitted by us. The sickening stench was terrible. Reverend Graham was soon overcome, and wanted to get out. We did not blame him. When we left it Marable's head was still above the head of the barrel as shown in the picture and Chris Baker threw himself upon it to further force it back into the receptacle. Marable's clothes were nowhere in sight. His arms and legs had been punctured. It was a ghastly sight the like of which we hope never to see again.

"How did this fiasco, I mean...?" Dr. McGuire sputtered.

"Yes sir, and as you can see, Mitchell, the editor, is something of a draftsman as well. Note that the caption on his sketch makes clear the address, on the off chance that some dim soul or newcomer in all the city may not know the exact location of the Medical College, or may confuse it with our institute on Clay.

"And his second sketch offers proof that this depredation was visited upon a Negro, his signature attached for verification."

Solomon Marable as he appeared in the barrel, after repeated efforts had been made to pull him out of it and he had to be left until the next morning.

"In truth, though, sir, this treatment, or worse, is the plight of every corpse that comes our way."

"And has been since antebellum times. The problem being that, for the people, what goes on in our anatomy laboratories has been but rumor and folk tale. But now.

"When I left their employ, I beseeched Taylor and Tompkins to put their house in order. They will need to ring the building with constables, I'm afraid. What, pray tell, was Matthews thinking?"

"I wonder that, too. School is out until October. The Medical College has no refrigeration. If the story told here is correct, then old Chris had made no gesture towards embalming the body, beyond salting it down like a side of pork. And this rush to compress the corpse in a barrel?"

"My guess is that Matthews and Baker intended to ship this material elsewhere, hoping to get it on the train and make their few dollars before the editor could find them. Are they so skint as to need those few coins? This article, these sketches, the people now see plainly what our trade entails. I must go to Matthews and confront him. This condemnation will fall on us, too. Will you go and warn Baker, tell him to stay inside? We must provide for him underground until this blows over. I fear, though, that we are in for a long trial."

CHAPTER 42

1898

TOO HOT TO DO MUCH, May like August this year. Had his whole rounds to run, though, slop up the rot and dump it. Baker had finished his janitorial duties at the Institute, tile floors gleaming and every knife and scalpel sharpened and stowed, but he'd barely begun with the Egyptian building cutting rooms, and couldn't crack a window for fear the stench would seep out or a rock get in.

The heat from the lye vat didn't help. He couldn't stir for long, had to back off and sit his father's old rocker to catch his breath. Thirty years, he thought, been at it alone all these years since Daddy died. He almost felt grateful when a slow rumble of thunder reached his ears. He lit his pipe that had been his father's, too, but let it go out in his hand. Sat waiting. Thirty years of storms and what they did to him. He'd fall, eyes rolling, and like as not awaken some timeless eon later clear on the other side of the room. He expected to go there now, heeding that first warning rumble upriver. Clutched the rocker arms tight and mumbled some fretful things that might have been a prayer, if he'd ever learned to pray.

Martha did it, she'd taught their son Johnny, and he'd tried it himself, because she insisted, and it was so pretty when they got down on their knees at bedside. So many things she wanted him to do that he couldn't. Why'd he bring that on her, let her make him her project? Just another one of her charity cases, most troubling one of all, and no way out of it now. The money was adding up, so she said. They could try to get that house, but he'd never live in it, not the way they'd dreamed it anyway. No more parading around like a family, too much risk in all that. What Martha did, in her work, and in her charity activities with Maggie Walker, and what Johnny did at school, that all took place on another planet, and he'd only hear about it in a couple hours maybe once a month on a moonless night, when he'd dare the dodge from lamp post to lamp post, tip-toeing up the loft stairs, then sneaking back to one college or the other long before sunup.

It was the Marable case that had cinched it, half the city marching on the Egyptian building, even tried to set the place afire. He'd cowered in the basement, new janitor they'd brought in for cleaning bringing him cheese and biscuits and sometimes a jar of soup, then scurrying up the steps like he feared he'd catch disease. Had to wait until the moon went down to race across the street to the new college, only to be imprisoned there, camping out in a broom closet, until another night when he could sneak back the other way.

The new anatomy law helped, bodies from the alms house and penitentiary dropped at the back door every week of the winter, but even so, the colleges were growing fast with more students every year; seemed like they never had enough stiffs to go around, so he still had to dig. Sometimes alone, pushing a wheelbarrow all the way out to Oakwood on the east end of town. Grates in the street and alleys he could hide in along the way, if need be. But one other thing about the new law, no protection if he did get arrested; they'd put him under the jail-house next time.

And poor Angel. What she needed was a daylight man like Maggie's, could sit a church pew nodding in pride as she sang up there in the choir loft. Johnny needed some kind of daddy he could claim, not pretending to have no father at all, hoping his classmates and their meddling parents would eventually forget the connection, especially those times another newspaper story came out playing him up as the devil himself. They sure didn't need the man they had. If one of them bullets had got him, right between the eyes, even if they'd strung him up from a tree. But here he squatted in the same dark cell, shivering as the storm came on, beset by the nattering of the haints at his ears now that he'd slowed down enough to listen. The half a skeleton he'd been threading rattled on its hook, and the arms of the old rocker creaked at the squeeze of his fingers.

His daddy had done a kind of praying, and all the way back, his mama did, too. Up on the school roof of a full moon. Where was that bag of pebbles they'd spread around up there? Couldn't have walked off by itself. Maybe the old woman had snatched it up again. She was out in the woods, like as not, shacked up from the storm, or who knows, she might be out on a bare knoll somewhere, rain-buffeted, baying at the wind. But she was close. Just yesterday had opened the back door to find a peeled bundle of roots at his feet. She knew how to do it, this solitary life. If only she'd show him how. It was summer he hated most. Students gone, back to straight up janitoring, half a day's work with the new man. Then you just sat. Almost made him yearn for that slap of thunder. Well, yearn or not, it would come.

"Fuck it." He said the words aloud, stood from the rocker and set off. Climbed the front steps to the lobby he'd swabbed just that morning, and kept on up to the infirmary ward, where he caught a nurse's eye on the stair. She hissed before turning her back. Winded already, he trod up past the empty offices, a row of locked doors, professors having run as far as they could from this place as soon as term ended, and at last reached the anatomy theater dim beneath a skylight pelted by rain. He leaned hard into the rooftop door and fell onto a flat tin roof pounding like drums. Where was it, where was that spot where they used to spread their circle of pebbles? Over there, near the Southeast corner, the one they'd said pointed to home.

Already drenched to the bone, his boots squishing, he fought the torrent to that spot and bent a long minute, hands on knees and gasping, rain like needles to his back. He remembered they called to the same Jesus as Martha did but also to another name he couldn't recall. This corner looked straight down on the jailyard, where the scaffold shook, skeletal in the storm. "Who was it y'all talked at, Mama?" he called. "Where you put that pebble bag?"

Upriver, a bolt of lightning split like shiny fingers down on Hollywood Hill, its sky-wide rumble mingling with the rooftop drum. "You want some, come and get it," he whispered, water streaming down his upturned face. "Here I stand, you want it. I ain't run no more."

CHAPTER 43

MAGGIE WALKER'S VISIT

OUT AT THE penitentiary a woman could interlace her fingers with her man's through the bars for ten minutes until the bell rang once a week. Free men signed on to work the tobacco fields upriver all Summer or portered the trains to New Orleans or Boston. Those that sailed a steamer out of Norfolk might trace the round world gone a year. Itinerant preachers had no home at all. So Martha Baker plainly knew that she was not the only woman warming her bed with a stove brick in a towel. One difference, though. Even the penitentiary wives could let on they had a husband somewhere. They swapped tales of pain and forbearance while slinging wet sheets on a line. Mrs. Baker laid low on all that, had learned to cut a sharp eye at anybody who asked, until eventually nobody dared. It was like her sole friend Maggie said, her man's lonely way was hers, too, now. She bore it the best she could.

The laundry women had shunned Martha once, some of them still sniffed, but all agreed that something had changed about their companion since her return from the country. Though she went back to singing in the church choir and resumed her charitable work, no one had seen her in the company of Chris Baker for years. Perhaps, they thought, she'd finally seen fit to send that scoundrel packing. Maybe in that early time, he'd held some kind of spell over her, a spell broken by all their earnest prayers, and now that she was free, the good Lord had spread his bounty about her, charged her with entrepreneurial zeal, and wasn't she a good boss woman, ran her crew like they was her own family, and paid them straight up, too.

Martha beamed with pride over her son Johnny. He'd never quit school despite the way they'd bullied him, and now was bringing in his own pay, laboring at the poor folks hospital on Clay Street that they called Sheltering Arms. Nobody teased him there; nobody seemed to make the connection to his hated father. Indoor work, but nonstop. He swabbed the messy floors, stoked the stoves, helped the ambulatory get around, restrained the frantic, spoon-fed the weak, and hefted the deceased, whatever needed doing. His mother urged him to move out of the loft, get his own place and get on, but he couldn't bear to think of her alone and unprotected if the people mobbed up again.

He saved the newspaper clippings, awoke from his pallet in the corner to greet his father on those infrequent midnight visits, and found himself straying after work down by the colleges, lurking at an advantageous corner in the vain hope that maybe he'd glimpse the man through a window or catch him passing on the street. Who was this character, after all, that they told such tales about? How could he match up the tired old man with the pipe, face lit by a lantern, who came and went in the dark, to the scandalous accusations in the papers?

Johnny stared up at the tall windows of the college on Clay, at the odd casements of the Egyptian Building off Marshall, but he never dared to announce himself. His mother's injunction - don't you ever cross that threshold — was his law. He could not imagine ever walking through those doors.

Over the years, the pillowcase that was their bank had graduated to a larger burlap feed sack, then a second one. The old cat patrolled, but Martha set traps in the closet, too, to keep mice from making confetti beds of the bills. She had hauled those sacks to the country and back again to the stable loft, and each week added to them from her laundry earnings and the pockets full of money her husband brought on his midnight visits. When she had filled a third sack, she invited Maggie to come see, if she would, and tell her if it might at last be possible.

Maggie took her own sweet time. She was so busy now, not just with her committee work and her position as leader of the St. Luke charitable organization, but also in inaugurating her grand, audacious dream, the founding of a penny bank for the Black community, which she saw as the culmination of a lifetime's effort on behalf of the city's freedmen and women.

Martha asked Johnny to join her at the kitchen table when Maggie finally arrived. Regal as the Queen of England, she nearly tripped on her satin gown coming up the stairs, but Johnny took her hand and her parasol to help her along. Martha had baked a paw paw cake and heated Maggie's favorite sassafras tea, served in the swirly-patterned china she'd purchased just for this occasion. The two friends greeted each other with cheek kisses, Maggie took in the two rooms, still sparsely furnished, the walls somewhat brightened by whitewash, and settled herself at the window.

"Dr. Watkins has treated you decently here?" she asked.

"He's gettin' on, more decrepit every day it seems. If he goes, don't know who'll take over this farm."

"Well, Martha, isn't it wonderful? This will no longer be your concern."

"Johnny counted it all, and it's stacked on the bed right now for you to see."

"In truth, you do our bank a favor, Martha, investing it all with us. The loan in your name, and best of all, the town house on St. Peter Street we discussed? Just down the lane from my own? We must go by there, a prim two-story in the Greek Revival style, has a cast iron porch, too. My husband Armstead has had his eye on it for you. Was a way station on the Underground Railroad they speak of, with a special feature that may be of use."

"Special feature?" Martha asked.

"Kitchen floor has a door to a hole in the ground, can sit up in there, nobody would know. You will not need it, but then...."

"Yes," Martha said, "I see."

"Do keep back some of your savings to furnish the place, but with your mark on these papers, it shall be yours."

"Where is this, again?" Johnny asked.

"Just off Clay Street, a short walk from your work, son, is what you want to know. Armstead put in a discrete side door on the alley, too. Safer for your daddy when he comes."

"This was his dream. Shame he can't be here today," Martha mused.

"We'll get word to him. Now come on, Johnny, bag up all your bounty and bring it out to my new victoria carriage, will you? Your days of mucking the stall below us will soon lie in the past."

CHAPTER 44

1903

THE SICKLE-SHAPED MOON hung low over Jackson Ward as Baker made his furtive way towards home. He slipped in at the gate on St. Peter Street and down the alley between houses to the side door, where he switched out of his stinking work clothes and into the denim slacks and linen shirt left waiting for him on the porch. Mrs. Baker greeted him in the kitchen with a swift kiss, offered a seat, and brought him calf's liver and onions kept warm on the wood stove.

They had not seen each other in a month, the weather clear and the moon bright at night. But he'd hung a white handkerchief as their signal on the flag pole over the college building that morning, ready to take a chance. She knew he would stay only an hour or two, creeping back to the college before the first hint of dawn.

"Here," he said, handing over a bulging leather purse, "This come in since I seen you last."

She pulled open the purse strings and poured out paper bills and coins, then sat counting them while he finished a dessert of bread pudding with butter sauce.

"You ain't need to count all that now," he said.

"You're right, husband, we have more than enough, always."

"This is it, ain't it?" he mused. "I 'member the first time we talked about a house for you."

"For you, too, Chris. If you would only come and stay. In the parlor, a rocking chair just for you by the fireplace hearth. We have our own bedroom upstairs, and another one for Johnny, just like we always said."

"How little man doin'?" he asked.

"Big man, you mean. Ask him yourself. He insisted on staying up to see you."

At that, Baker's son, who had been waiting in the parlor, stepped forward, his figure nearly filling the doorway. Always a surprise somehow to see how he'd sprouted up so fast.

"Daddy," he asked, "You seen the streetcar yet?"

"Hear it sometimes."

"I ride it, Daddy! Just to get on and off. No horse to pull it, there's electric wires strung along, and that's what makes it go."

"Ain't have no truck with 'lectricity," Baker frowned.

"It's fun, Daddy. Makes an awful racket, though, so the horses buck."

"Streetcar, is it? Ain't even seen the new city hall they talk about."

"Well, it's right there plain as day on Broad Street. You could hit it with a rock from the college."

"I go by there sometime, take a look."

"You stay clear of Broad Street, Mr. Baker, you know what's good for you," his wife warned.

"Daddy," the young man said, "Been wanting to show you something. Did some calculating on your work."

"Calculatin'? What you got there?"

His son pulled a sheet of paper from his pants pocket and unfolded it. "Added up the stiffs you been getting this year. It's a lot."

"Cain't count past my fingers, Johnny, how you figure all this?"

"Well, look here. You tell Mama when you come how many you got this week, and then I stretch that out to the weeks when you don't come, so here's what I figured."

"Where'd you learn all this, Johnny? You some kind of scientist?"

"Book learnin', Mr. Baker. What the normal school taught him," his wife replied proudly.

"So look at this, Daddy." Johnny spread the paper open on the table, and traced each line with a finger as he explained.

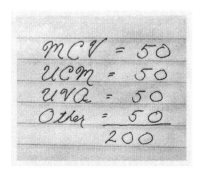

"Now school year at the college is 34 weeks, am I right? So that means you need to be getting five or six bodies a week to keep everybody supplied. Did I figure that right?"

"Load from the penitentiary, from the poor house, asylums, too, come in pretty regular."

"That's a lot of dead people, Daddy."

"And be needin' more. Both schools here addin' on a year plus more freshmen every term. Weren't for all these fevers and the consumption, man couldn't keep up."

"You still workin' the graveyards, Daddy?"

"Johnny, hush," Mrs. Baker said.

"That ain't stop, no. Cain't keep up without it," he sighed.

"Funny thing, though," Mrs. Baker said. "Other day Maggie allowed she might still be teaching school if it wasn't for what you do."

"How is that?"

"Say she got that idea for her first big project, a burial society, so people could pay by the month, afford a secure casket and a vault, when they gone."

"Shoot, that ain't the half of all she do."

"Well seems to me, if you stopped all this digging tonight, people would still want their mort-safes and vaults, it's a habit to them now. Everybody can pay a penny a week wants it. But I worry for you, Chris. You can't keep on like this."

"Anybody stop in this house, it's you and that laundry."

"No, husband, that's the thing." She pulled her chair closer, leaned in and took his hand. "Had a meeting with Maggie, we'd hoped you could get free to come."

"She up in her penny bank and all, still make time for us?"

"She offered me work there, or in the department store she's putting in on the ground floor."

"Well that's somethin'. Who take on all your laundry business, one a your girls?"

"That's why I wanted to see you so bad, see what I did, and you can talk me out of it, turned her offer around. Take out a second loan on the house, buy one of the new steam washers, and can double my business at half the labor. Johnny added it up and Maggie says he got the numbers right, too."

Baker turned his wife's hand in his, examining her strong fingers and work-thickened wrist, the sheen of her arms blanched by a life up to her elbows in bleach and lye soap.

"Just seem like more work to me," he frowned.

"We worked it out, and if we get it right, the machines will do the washing, and pay for themselves. Like Maggie says, you got to keep up. If we don't do it, somebody will."

"And if it don't work, she take this house?"

"It will work, husband. And see, this is the thing. What this means is, you can stop. Just the laundry alone can do for us."

"Me stop? My college work?"

"Listen to me, if they catch you with that digging law and lock you up, who says the new governor will let you out this time?"

"That law don't bother me. Dr. McGuire at the institute, his daddy was Stonewall Jackson's surgeon in the war. White folk think he's God. And Taylor at the college, man's the city coroner, they ain't mess with him."

"All those chemicals, the fumes, they work on you, Chris."

"What it do to me now? Already pickled pretty good."

"Do you remember the fresh air in the country, how you loved that sweet breeze?"

"Go back to the preacher's, is that it?"

"We could do that, too. They looked up to you there. What you did for his daughter, and his mama, too."

"Word travel from down this way, though, where we run then?"

"You know what I think, Daddy?" their son interrupted. They'd almost forgotten he was there.

"What you think, Johnny?" Baker asked, dropping his wife's hand.

"I think you like it, your job."

Baker considered this a moment, then replied, "Thing is, you ain't known him, but your grandaddy say a man find somethin' he can do, he ought to keep at it."

Johnny nodded, having heard this line before. He refolded his notes and tucked them in a pocket.

"Paper called you the ghoul of Richmond, Daddy."

"Paper say a lot of things."

"You ain't no ghoul to me."

"Whatever they call me, just leave it be, son. The work I do stop with me."

Mrs. Baker got up to clear away the empty plates and the bag of money, saying, "Get on now, Johnny. You got work tomorrow. Daddy see you next time he comes."

Reluctantly, Johnny turned away and climbed the stairs to his room. Mrs. Baker waited until she heard his door close, then took her seat, gazing for a long moment at her husband's tired face, before saying what she really meant: "They're going to kill you, Chris. Counted forty empty graves in Oakwood Cemetery and *The Planet* stirring people up again, like before we went to the country."

"What I'm gonna do, though? Cain't just stop."

"Have you been listening to my plan at all? It's all to get you out of that stinky old college basement."

"You think they ever stop gunnin' for me? This fine home you got here with Johnny, they come burn it to the ground."

"I'ma take that loan."

"Didn't doubt it."

"Oh, Chris," she pleaded, "You could quit, you could let all that death work go. But you won't, I see that in the set of your jaw."

Mrs. Baker stood and went to the window, pulled back the shade just enough for a glimpse out to the darkened alley, and mused, "No you won't. And my question for you, sir, is why?"

CHAPTER 45

TATE'S BARBER SHOP - 1906

"WE GOT THAT FUCKER, we got 'im!"

Tate the barber leaped from his chair and tugged down the window shades. "Get away Jack, what you bring that shotgun in here for?"

The disheveled intruder slammed the door and fell back against it, a heavy gun drooping in his arms. "Naw, Tate, he went down, I'm tellin' you."

"Boy, what you come here for? Police on you out there?"

"Got to stow this gun! You got to take it from me, Tate!"

"Get in here, Jack, lock that door. Come in back here a minute so I can knock you upside the head good one time."

The two men hurried to the back pantry and huddled there behind a curtain hung on the door.

"Alright," the barber said, "Take this bottle and drink it down. Now tell me what y'all did."

Jack set down the shotgun and took a long swig, then slumped against the wall and let out a sigh. He shook his head, as if just beginning to grasp the gravity of it all, and whispered, "What we talked about. Ambushed that grave robbin' fool right outside the college. Seen him go down and boy did we lit out from there!"

"Baker you talkin' 'bout? You shot Chris Baker?"

"Well, Skippy did is what I figure. I ain't got off a round. But heard the shot and watched him fall. Now I got to get rid this gun!"

"Wait a minute, catch your breath, you did what?" The barber retrieved the bottle and took a gulp, then pulled back the curtain a notch to watch the front door.

"Alright, here, this how it went. We had him boxed in good. Ain't no potshot through a window, this a straight up ambush out the war. And nobody say we ain't had the right to do it neither. You know it! Them doctor schools wrestlin' with families at the poor house for a body, jail got standin' orders, and you cain't lay down at Oakwood he ain't dug you up already. That is one busy snatcher, ain't he? Workin' both colleges now.

"So we figure, he gotta come out sometime, least to get that old ambulance and head up cemetery way, and when he do, we lay the hammer down. Anywhere he run, one of us got him. So Skip had his carbine, shoot a fly off a stump at half a mile. Wife work at the hospital by old man McGuire's school, so he climb up on the roof there with line of sight down Clay. Fire straight down if he come out the front door. Ronnie had his Colt revolver, and say fuck it, just walked right up to that nasty Egyptian mausoleum he work in, post up behind one of them fat columns by the front door. I say he ain't come out that way, he ain't that dumb, but Ronnie say whatever he do, he chase him down.

"I took my spot by the privy at the old Davis White House, in between them schools, got a clear look across the playground there. This here 12-gauge, one of them barrels take him down for sure. Any way he come out, one of us get him, and my bet was on me. Now Missy, my girl, she a maid at the boardin' house some of them students stay at, let on they low on bodies this week, so we figure that old snatcher be hungry. Police cain't keep him out the graveyards, we put him down 'fore he ever get there."

"Boy, police catch you with that shotgun, put *you* in the graveyard!"

"Least now my old body can rest there, ain't it? Chris Baker ain't diggin' no more."

"What were y'all thinkin', Jack? Station house jes' down the hill, too. And them tales, how he a conjure man, strike you down with a look or raise you up from the dead with a kiss of his foul lips. Ronnie's old bullshit, turn a bullet in the air and all that."

"Yeah, yeah, heard it all. Let's see if this little tippy devil can turn a volley back is what we said. Set up after dark, pretty evenin' last night, won't it? We just sit. Not a man in our posse but wants to be the one put him down. No moon, constable go by regular, but you know Black or white neither, people ain't go up that way at night. But he ain't come. Eyes gettin' heavy, sky gettin' light, we got to get home before sunup, out on the street with these guns. But then, just when I was 'bout ready to whistle 'em off, here he come, Lucifer hisself, stridin' sharp out the front door of McGuire's school there on Clay.

"You ever seen that man? He ain't nothin' but a little roly-poly fellow, all dressed in black, look like a fat shadow crossin' that playground, and at a sporty clip, too."

The barber nodded, "You'd hustle yourself, you been picked at like he has. Gotta say, I do have a twinge of pity for that fool."

"Little bit a that come on me, too, layin' up there all night. But then I think a Mama, she ain't long for this world. Cousin Cholley in the pen. That all the stiffenin' my backbone required.

"Had a clean shot, too, level and true, was linin' up to hit him with both barrels, aim right at his big ol' pumpkin head, and blam! Gotta been Skip, think I seen a muzzle flash up on the roof. Then I see Ronnie take off round the corner, look back, and Baker is down! Skip got that fucker, boy!

"Knew one thing, that gunshot wake up the police, so I cleared outta there, hid in the bushes till I seen you come in. You got to take this gun, I got to find my boys, and they got to shut they chops. We done it now, Tate, we done it!"

"Preacher praise your names from the pulpit, Jack."

"You keep quiet, Tate. We all hang they find out who done this."

"Well, I ain't seen you today. Go out the back fence. Leave that gun. But I mean, damn! Mystery boys done got Chris Baker. If that don't make a headline!"

"Two of the freshmen found him crumpled at the threshold to the building, sir, a trail of blood up the steps, and he thrashing about something awful! Please come!"

Dr. Tompkins set down his magnifying glass and looked up from his notes at the student panting at his office door. He shook his head sadly, "A target on his back, poor man. We all knew, one day, they'd get him." Grabbing his gladstone bag, he shooed the student down the steps and strode briskly along Marshall Street to the college. Shot outside, he silently fretted. If only we'd finished that tunnel we promised him.

"You say Baker's been shot at before?" the student asked.

"Have you not seen the bullet holes perforating the college windows?"

"Oh, I thought from the war. How does he stand it, this work?"

"One might wonder, indeed. No telling, really, what a life enveloped in the corruptions of decay and the chemicals of preservation may have done to this man. Baker risks his life each time he steps outside, yet puts on a show of cheer, never lets on that he has a care in the world. I witnessed the same bravado amongst seasoned troops during the war; whistling past the graveyard, we called it."

The student grinned, "Well Ol' Chris has done his whistling *inside* the graveyard, often as not."

"It is not a thing to make light of," Dr. Tompkins chided. "We old soldiers, our burden has never lifted, though our whistling has stopped. Baker's war persists, it seems, a target and an outcast, immured in that abattoir that has served as his living tomb."

"Is he entirely alone, sir?"

"Well, a wife, a son I believe, and a house of some sort in the Jackson Ward."

"He doesn't go there?"

"On rare occasions, I believe. He would not have them become targets, as he is."

"Our maid at the boarding house has mentioned her fear of him. Says mothers call their children inside at night, threatening kidnap by him they call the night doctor."

"One of the kinder appellations given our friend, I'm afraid. Listen, whatever happens, I must charge you to do this. When the newspapermen come, and they surely will, do not tell them what happened. We cannot allow the public to know there was a shooting."

"What will I tell them?"

"Say he was taken ill, something of that nature. Anything but this."

They reached the college building and stepped around a trail of blood on the steps. Inside, Baker lay sprawled on the vestibule floor, two students crouching at his side, helplessly watching blood pool beneath him. Bending to his longtime janitor, Dr. Tompkins gripped his hand, before reaching in his bag for scissors to cut away his pants leg. "Shot to the thigh, I think, Chris. Let's just hope the slug hasn't nipped your femoral artery."

"What you do, doctor?" Baker whispered.

"We've got to operate, now, Chris. Can take you straightway upstairs to the infirmary."

"Don't put me out, Doctor. Don't do that to me, please," he gasped.

"The chloroform is short acting, Chris. The surgery will be intolerable without it, I'm afraid. Allow us to comfort you in the act."

"Ain't that. You cain't leave me in a room with other folk, if I cain't get up and get away."

Dr. Tompkins paused for a moment, considering whether Baker's fear was reasonable or simply the habit of his paranoia. Well, the proof was the bullet in his leg, after all.

"Alright, we shall conduct this surgery in the dissection theater, and you may recover downstairs on your pallet. May I contact your wife to nurse you here?"

"She ain't come down here," he moaned.

"Then I shall nurse you myself. The sooner we get on with this, the sooner you will be out of your pain."

"Up in the dissection room? You lay me down on one a them cuttin' tables?"

"Yes, Chris, there," the doctor smiled. We can ponder that irony another time."

THE STORY MADE the front pages of all seven local newspapers and as far away as Staunton and Washington, DC, but none mentioned a shooting, only that "Dr." Chris Baker had required surgery for a sudden illness, and seemed to be recovering nicely.

For instance this headline from the *Richmond News Leader*, September 3rd:

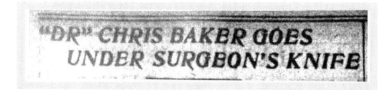

"DR" CHRIS BAKER GOES
UNDER SURGEON'S KNIFE

But around the city of Richmond, rumors swelled. Anybody with an ear knew he'd been shot, and who did the shooting, too. Fell dead on the street is what they said. And what that meant was what people feared most, some old talk from the old country. Words like boogeyman, vampire, zombie, revenant, demon. Death walker.

CHAPTER 46

1908

MARTHA BAKER TOOK her usual shortcut through the Shockoe Hill Cemetery towards the alms house at its northern border, the institution's stolid brickwork front so like a prison's. At times this walk could be a stroll, the graveyard a sort of park, but today she hurried, because the belt on one of the new washing machines had shredded. She hauled its heavy replacement across her shoulder. The salesman had made great claims for the machine, but sometimes it seemed that she spent more time repairing these labor-saving behemoths than her staff might have spent scrubbing by hand with washboards.

She did notice, however, the dawning beauty of this early spring day, frost on the lawn melting to glistening dew and a troop of robins flitting among the tombstones, so busy in their hunt for thawing worms that they barely paused to sing. She knew his figure at once, a slumped shadow standing just outside the eastern wall, near the old blasted sycamore stump. What was he doing out, in broad daylight? She looked around, hoping they were alone, then turned and stepped off the bricked walkway, making her way to him through the graves.

"Mr. Baker," she called.

He turned to her, a little sheepishly, then smiled and opened his arms to her embrace.

"Surprised to find you out of a morning, sir," she said.

He took the rubber belt from her shoulder and tried to stretch it between his hands. "Oh, Mama call me out here, come after dark, been here now I reckon all night. Guess the sunup caught us at it."

"Talk with your Mama, is it? Would have liked to hear that."

"This old stump, you 'member it?"

"I do indeed, my husband."

"Mama tell me this old dead tree here, take just as long as it stood for it to rot away to dirt. Well on its way, too, but look here, these old dead limbs white as bones been laid out here in the graveyard all these years since that storm. Nobody took a stick of it for firewood nor thought to clear it away."

"It's your daddy. What happened that night. People say the devil took that tree."

"They still talk that way, don't they? Remember Ol' Billie."

"And you, too, Chris. You can't stay out here long."

"We was talkin' 'bout how it don't take a man but a week to get ripe. Seen 'em melt down to a puddle if you leave 'em too long. Don't know how long it take a bone to rot. Maybe longer than this old tree."

"You out here all night with these ponderings?"

"Mama say she grateful to finally come out here, see where my daddy lay. Made her that promise a long ways back."

"She said that, did she?" Mrs. Baker looked deeply into her husband's bloodshot eyes, then took a measured few steps back. "Come to me," she said.

He let the heavy belt drop, stepped towards her, and as she suspected, one toe seemed to drag. The arm on that side hitched at the elbow.

"You know you're hobblin', Chris?"

He took her hand, unable to meet her gaze. "It's just that ol' bullet got me. Was a cold night, got stiff. Loosen up hereabouts."

That wasn't it, of course. She had seen the dragging stride and cocked arm of a stroke victim many a time at the alms house and the hospital.

"You have a cane?" she asked.

"Ol' hickory stick, yeah. Ain't all that bad."

"When can you come home?"

"Get over there 'fore long. They 'bout done with term. You keep a light on, look for my flag."

"Johnny sure would like to see you."

"I get over there – real soon."

"What does she look like, your Mama?"

"Ain't you ever seen her? She right here. Say hello, Mama. This my Angel."

"It's just us here, Chris. Don't go on like that."

"Oh, she step off again. Got no manners a'tall, that woman."

"Chris."

For a long moment, she hugged him. Then she bent and lifted the washing machine belt to her shoulder. "Listen, husband, you best go on back to that college building, before the sun gets too high."

"Naw, you go on – I be alright."

She turned away, almost tripping on a plot of sunken grass. Unmarked, for protection from vandals, but she knew. All those years ago, that daring choice, she'd bent to a forlorn figure, soaked with rain. For a moment she felt dizzy, almost as if unseen hands tugged at her dress. No, she thought, one of us must keep their head on straight; one of us must hold on.

He stood before his father's grave and watched her dwindle towards the alms house. "She think I'm crazy," he whispered.

It took him by one ear this time and jerked his head around, so he spun in a full circle, falling hard onto his back. He stared up in mild surprise at the empty blue sky and a palimpsest of bare limbs that had traced the air in days past. He called out or may have just thought the word in his momentary confusion: "Mama?"

Across the broad lawn of the tombstone-spiked cemetery, dew-sparkling and robin-livid, no answer came.

CHAPTER 47

1910

HE PULLED the old rocker up close to the wood stove and crossed his bare feet before it, blue with cold. The low ceiling sagged along its cracks, shadows wavering in the firelight. A narrow escape this time. Had gone out alone, no student willing to face the blizzard, and the drifts too deep for the ambulance, so he'd unbolted the wheels from his barrow, harnessed himself with a rope across his chest, and pulled it along like a sled all the long trudge out to Oakwood cemetery on the far east edge of town. At end of term, when all the colleges needed fresh stiffs for their final exams, there never seemed to be enough coming in legal from the prisons and poor houses, always one or two short. He trudged an extra mile on a side route to the pauper's field, but caught sight of a constable, who waited at the gate while he labored with the shovel.

The disinterment came easy, a shallow burial for one of the old tramps who lurked around the depot coughing their lungs out with consumption or worse. They'd buried him nude, every strip of his clothing on somebody's else's back now. That they'd bothered to nail together a matchstick coffin came as a surprise. But sparse as he was, he popped up easy from the hole, dragged out by a rope looped under his arms. Turning him onto the tarp, Baker caught himself, his hands feeling along rough welts scored across the man's back. "Old Grandpa," he said, "What they did to you? Boys have to come at you from the front, knife won't cut through all that."

Driving snow had reblanketed the man's grave by the time he had the body tarp-wrapped and tucked onto the sled, but he continued his one-way conversation, as he crouched there waiting out the constable.

"Never took the whip to me, old man. Always done what they told me, just about. Holed up in that college all my years. What all you seen out there in the world, got you tore up like that?"

Baker and the policeman, not a hundred yards apart, traded hacking coughs through the blustery night. Before first light, though, the officer waved and shrank away, defeated. Baker shook off the snow, and made his way home, pulling the sled on a zig zag route through back alleys, and rousing all the dogs of Church Hill to barking as he went. His weak leg never helped much, but it had all but given out by the time he got to the Shockoe gulch. He stumbled downhill in knee-deep drifts, leaning into the snow-laden wind sweeping down the gorge. He knew that police patrolled the main cross streets and the new viaduct that cut through the old Negro burying ground, so he set out across the maze of train tracks in the bottom, aiming as best he could towards the college building on the opposite ridge.

A long coal train, parked on a siding, blocked his way. It looked like a black wall in the otherwise blanched landscape. On his knees, he shoved the sled between the wheels of one car, then lay face down on the tracks under the train for a long while, pleading with his pounding heart to slow, and grateful for a bit of shelter from the biting storm. Between coughing fits, he told the corpse of the old days, when the only thing down in this holler was graves and garbage and a stinky old creek, and he asked the man which one of the slave markets along the bottom he might have been sold out of.

"Took my mama day 'fore Christmas, Grandpa. I's just a little boy. You ever seen her in your roamin'? She's somethin' to behold. You'd surely 'member her."

At last he climbed back onto his feet and stared up at the steep slope ahead. When he re-tied the rope around his waist and headed uphill, the body kept sliding off the sled, so he had to regroup, get around behind the thing, and shove the sled along on his knees, one heave at a time. Halfway up, he paused to catch his breath and sprawled atop the corpse, his heels dug in so they wouldn't slide. It would take nothing, he knew, to let the snow cover him there, and why not, after all?

It was his phlegm-filled lungs that saved him. The hacking and wheezing, his father's rheumy cough, resumed. It shook him upright and got him going again, fueling his final push to the top. He shoved the back door open and fell into the basement, dragged the corpse inside just far enough to shut the door again, then forced himself to crawl across the floor to the old rocker, where he summoned one last hacking gasp to stoke the stove. The only way he knew to calm the cough was to sit the rocker, tipping up and back with hands on knees, his body quaking, until his throat burned raw and tears streamed down his face.

When the eruption at last subsided, his head fell back. After a while, he dozed. When he awoke, a human skull rested on his knee, and one hand held a long femur bone. He didn't remember picking them up, but so many things these days seemed to come and go on their own. His clothes were drenched, the stove needed tending, day coming on, but he lolled in a revery for the longest time, tapping the skull with the bone as if that tender drumming might explain what he'd put himself through, might call up and make plain those answers that danced just the other side of his knowing. Which, to his surprise, now came.

You ain't do it fo' dem Fessor Doctors. Bigger hand in it den all dat.

It was the old grandpa. While he slept, the emaciated corpse had somehow pulled itself free of its tarp wrapping, and now sat propped upright against the lye vat in the middle of the floor.

"Say what?" he whispered.

The dead man's leathery jaw lisped back at him, *Down my way, folks call him Ol' Plat-eye. What y'all call him?*

Baker startled then at a restless settling of ashes in the stove. The room seemed to breathe, expanding and contracting in a rhythm with his tapping on the skull.

"Ain't call him at all. Just came," he answered.

The cadaver's jaws chomped at that, shaping a kind of lipless grin.

You called him alright. First time you went diggin' in dem graves.

"You seen him, this Plat-Eye a yours?"

He what yo' Mama been after you 'bout, the corpse said.

"My mama? You seen her?"

Tap dat drum, boy. Call her up. See if she don't come.

"What you sayin', Grandpa? You sayin' she a haint?"

Hush, boy. Thing you ought know 'fore you go choppin' me up. Yo mama ain't kidnap like dem doctors say.

Baker sat upright at that.

Dem Fessor Doctors a yours? Sold yo' mama down de river. So's dey could buy a dray horse.

"What? That old horse they went and bartered in the war for some bushels of corn?"

Dat de one.

Baker's head seemed to ratchet about of its own accord, scanning the dingy cell. "How you know that?" he asked.

How a body know anything, the corpse replied. *Don't matter. Like I say, you ain't work fo' dem doctors no way.*

"Why you say that?"

Many a year been waitin' on you, boy. My luck to be de one, ain't it?

Bile dripped down the cadaver's chin as he spoke and his dry eyes scrolled up yellow in their sockets.

Well, you done now, Baker. Ain't no more diggin' fo' you. Mine de last grave you gon' rob in dis life. But you done pretty good. Tol' me tell you dat."

"Who told you? What?"

Tap dat drum now, tap it, boy. She come if she can.

The Interview

A long moment passed, that pregnant pause the young reporter guessed might lead to some more interesting admission. A clock tolled somewhere in the bowels of the building. So easy here to imagine oneself entombed in a pyramid, mummified bodies stirring. How could anyone bear to dwell in such a sarcophagus? He coughed into his scented handkerchief, which seemed to stir his thoughtful subject. At last the man spoke, this time at a measured pace, as if reading from a book:

"Since you here, they is one thing I want to say. People like to tell tales, like you will with mine. Well, fit this to your story, will you? Y'all bury your loved ones, so you say, out of respect. But that's not really why you go to so much trouble. It's all to turn your backs on what I know. The plain truth you don't want to see. Change your thinkin', too, if you ever dared to really take a gander. You buckle at the thought, but until you have the thing before you, mark its slow decay, see how the body sack is just only a balloon that swell and bust its seams and drain away, you ain't know what I know. Y'all want your dead in the ground and gone. Out of sight, out of mind, like they say. Call that respect. Tell yourself pretty tales. Fancy ideas that help you get some sleep. Alright. That all you can take, I let it go. But you ought to at least own up to it. Seem like y'all do owe me that."

CHAPTER 48

RETIREMENT CEREMONY - 1914

QUEER TO SEE the old doctors McGuire and Taylor on the same stage, back inside the Egyptian building where it had all started for both of them. But they'd shook hands on it now, the two medical schools coming together as one, the way they should have done all along. Baker well remembered the elderly gentlemen in their rowdy youth, as he recalled in some detail every one of the hundreds of students who had passed under his watch over the past half-century, earnest white boys squeamish at the cutting board, sometimes more than half the class dropping out before the winter term was done. The young Hunter McGuire had come in like a cavalry, bringing with him a trainload of Southern boys who'd been studying up north, leading them back in a huff when the rumors of war began to fly. And the Fessor Doctor back then had let them all study for free. Whole gang off to the battlefield before they'd ever won their degrees. McGuire was gone now, dead of a stroke at the century's turn, city shut down for three days in mourning. It was his son Stuart onstage tonight, spitting image of his warhorse dad, tall as a tree and eyes blue as marbles.

Old man Taylor was still at it, though, showing off his new

book about field hospitals in the war. How he'd dig up roots and drain tree sap for medicine when the supply lines were down. Odd-looking fellow, with those bottle-thick glasses and white nest of a beard, city coroner and world traveler – how many skeletons had Baker boiled down and strung up as gifts to European doctors for that man's cross-Atlantic journeys?

Baker was surprised to see the auditorium packed for this occasion. McGuire announced right up front that every one of the nearly 300 current students in the medical school, and in the new dental and pharmacy schools of the now combined Medical College of Virginia and University College of Medicine sat in the audience, and doctors from a lot of the previous classes, from both the college and the old institute had shown up, too. He gazed out at their faces from his place of honor on the stage, half-listening to the two Fessor Doctors jawing. Taylor had known him as a youngster, old Billie's shadow, had grown up in his practice same as young Chris. Worked side by side at the cutting table for many a year.

But he didn't know the half of all Baker had done. What it was like to lay up in a thicket, waiting out the constables at the graveyard on a long winter's night. He'd never jellied a cadaver down to skeleton, dug in the soup for bones; he'd never yanked teeth out of jaw bones for the barbers that they were putting out of the dental business with these fancy teachings at the new school. No one in the audience knew how to preserve rotting tissue in salt, or rum, or quicklime; how to embalm a body right or pickle a stiff in formaldehyde. All the ways of managing decay that had evolved across his time among the dead. Honored by the white folk and feared by the colored, they'd never caught a rock upside the head. Lived high on the hog in their fancy homes and slept with their families all safe and warm. So they'd been through the same times but not in the same way, though the way they talked this morning, you'd think they were all bosom friends.

The Board of Visitors had invited Baker to stay on in his quarters in the basement, as long as he continued to help out around the dissection lab from time to time. Wouldn't be easy to find a replacement for all he did. No Black man would take that job in this house of horrors. And no white would put up with all it required. New man wouldn't have to get out in the cemeteries, though. The good embalming they did now and all the bodies coming in from poor houses and asylums and jails all over Virginia on the refrigerator trains could about keep up with the needs of a four-year course of study for all them students. If they did find somebody, though, he'd promised to show him the ropes.

Martha and Johnny weren't there, of course. Nothing would change about that. He could get up to St. Peter Street on a moonless night sometimes, and stay a month now, all the curtains closed, if school was out. Martha limping, too, with a bad hip from all her years traipsing around town to her laundry works. Johnny grown, told him straight up, you ain't doin' this work, uh uh. But damned if he didn't keep it in the family anyway, left his bucket work at the hospital to take a job at Price's Funeral Home on Duval Street. He'd teased his father last time they'd been together, "I put 'em in the ground and you take 'em out again." It was steady work, they both agreed, never been and never would be no shortage of dead people.

When they were all together at home, it was heaven on a biscuit. But then he knew the doctors would call him back one night, need help with this or that, and then he was stuck again in the basement, never show his face. People didn't seem to want to forget. Rumors flew, and the stories grew more colorful the more they spread. Mrs. Baker said, "Everybody likes a good ghost story, Chris." He nodded, "Seem like everybody need a good whippin' boy, too." Which they both agreed he would be for all his days.

After a while, McGuire and Taylor ran out of steam and called him to speak. He helped himself up with his hickory cane and hobbled to the podium. The audience rose and cheered and clapped and hooted for the longest time. Some of the old boys had come along on his night doctoring adventures, some had never once dared touch a cadaver with a scalpel and graduated anyway. But they were all doctors now, cutting on the living.

These men were well aware that he knew some of the starkest things about them. That he had taught them lessons they never could have learned any other way, and much of that learning had been about who they were and could be. "Thank the Lord it's all behind us," the doctors confided to the students in their midst. "Be glad you weren't here in the old days!"

Baker said his thanks and wished them all well in their good works. There wasn't much more to say. It had always been his way to show instead of tell. So he waved a hand and turned from the podium.

Someone in the audience shouted, "What will you do now, Chris?" Was it a reporter in their midst, looking for a headline?

Baker paused, lifted his cane in both hands, the way you'd hold a ladle, and allowed that devilish grin as he demonstrated. "Oh, I be downstairs you come see me. Same as always, stirrin' the bones."

CHAPTER 49

JUNE 1919

"He's gone soft in the head, close as he is now. Wants me to bring up that old pallet from the college building he used to sleep on in the day."

"That raggedy thing? Well, bring it, then. If it will settle him down a bit. Can't hardly keep him in the bed. Every time the clock chimes, he rolls out, huffin' and mumblin'."

Baker's son went to the college building basement and looked around at the cramped and low-ceilinged workshop. So this was my daddy's world, he thought. Not so different from what we do at Price's, and at the same time, the opposite of all that, too. He swept up a row of dusty wooden carvings and brought them along back to the house with the pallet, saying, "Don't tell him yet – let me air this old thing out, smells like death itself."

Later he brought the pallet up to his father's bedroom and stretched it out on the floor, noting how the old man lifted his head from the pillow and looked around blindly, sniffing the air.

"Got your old pallet, Daddy, like you wanted. It's right here. You like, I can get you on it."

Baker nodded, so his son bent to him, lifted his legs off to the side of the bed and helped his father sit up, then pivoted him around and down to the old gray pallet on the floor. It had hardly any padding, the cotton bolls and straw pulled out long ago by mice making their nests in the basement eves, but as soon as the old man lay situated on his back, supported at the head by a good feather pillow, he seemed to calm a little. Johnny reached in the sack and pulled out a figurine shaped like a lion and fitted his father's stiff hands around it. That seemed to ease him, too. He lay there, breathing evenly now, his eyes closed as his gnarled gray hands fingered the wooden shape.

"I told Price if he wants me to stay on as his chief embalmer and beautifier, he needs to take my daddy, I don't care what the people say. Pourin' him a concrete vault and a steel coffin, too, lay him out at Evergreen," Johnny said.

"He never dug out that far, did he?" asked his mother.

"Never had to. By the time that cemetery got goin', had all the stiffs he needed legal from the state, and this past year, Lord, morgue can't keep up with the Spanish Flu."

"He had a job of work goin', though, didn't he?"

"He did that."

The old man's eyes opened then and he seemed to nod. He reached up but instead of taking his hand, his son dug in the sack and offered another figurine, this one an elephant with an S-curved trunk made, he guessed, of sycamore.

The young man and his mother did not see the other visitor, who had been there all along, plopped now in the middle of the empty bed. Its many hands rubbed its plump belly, the skulls at its belt clacked and chuckled, and the swarm of eyeballs atop its neck ogled about on their stringy stalks. Like the others, the monster waited.

And then its arms lifted and seemed to beckon. The room began to quiver and go foggy; the living there felt the house tremble. Baker's son shook his head, "That old mattress. I don't know. We got to open a window or somethin'. You can see the stink risin' in here."

But it was haints that shook the house, their gossamer presence an electrical shimmering, as they piled in shoulder to shoulder, when they still had shoulders, their dim images overlapping as the crowd came on, until they filled the room to the brim, and still they came, their phantom weight pressing upon the man on the pallet, feet treading his shallow chest. Disembodied hands crawled across the floor and teased his face and ears, jaws bereft of teeth nibbled at his bare toes, the bodies that still had heads droned like some factory machine, their dry throats humming one deep and sorrowful note, all in chorus.

Old Billie took a seat, cross-legged on the floor, smiling to see the wooden figurines in his son's hands. He was all of a piece, no digger had gotten to him after all, so he'd rotted whole like you should. Behind him stood his mother in her rough burlap gown, and behind her another old woman and another and a line of them stacked up out the door, craning forward as best they could. They all had those distant death walker eyes like Baker himself, his kin from way back in the homeland.

"Where you at now, boy, what you doin'?" his father asked.

"Oh Daddy, just walkin' the Shockoe Creek is all. Find Mama a shiny pin for Christmas."

Chris Baker, age 64, at front door of the Egyptian Building, Medical College of Virginia, 1914

Chris Baker on front step of Egyptian Building.

THE RICHMOND VIRGINIAN

MONDAY MAY 7, 1917

Excerpted from the article:

DEATH HOVERING OVER MYSTERIOUS "CHRIS"

―――――――

Old Negro Who Has Been in Care of Dissecting Room of Medical College Half a Century is Dying.

―――――――

FEARED BY ALL NEGROES

―――――――

Members of His Race Believed He Bore Charmed Life and Thought He Was a "Conjurer" - Tried to Kill Him.

―――――――

Death is about to claim the figure of Chris Baker, who in his time has been more closely associated with death, perhaps, than any other man in the history of the South. Chris has been for about fifty years connected with the Medical College of Virginia as caretaker of the "stiffs," and is well known to every doctor who has come out of the school since the Civil War. For twenty-five years he has been away from the college campus but once, it is said, since he is feared by the other members of his race with a horror equal to the dread of a fatal disease. He has been shot at scores of times, and negroes believe he bears a charmed life. He is now in the shadow of death, and it is doubtful if he will ever return to his habitual haunts again.

About himself he said little, but in the numerous decades of his pursuits among the dead he built up a philosophy of his own, which was not at all without its merits. He grew up in the dissecting room, and for years has been in charge of the college "stiffs," those cold, cheerless forms of the dead brought there to be displayed to teach young doctors, often by grim example, the means to combat the ravages of death. Then, as the years grew on, the awfulness of his life, in daily and nightly contact with these clammy, speechless forms, had its effect on the other members of his race, until he became surrounded with a mysterious cloud of supernatural import. Other negroes began to fear him, and to speak his name in whispers.

Wielder of Black Magic

This grew and grew, until rumors floated about concerning him and his practices. Children listened with wide-open eyes to stories of how "Ole Chris" talked with the dead, and knew the secrets of the grave, and all the other dread but fascinating things that are wrapped in the same hush that goes with superstition. Negroes feared him more and more, until they held him in such awe that they would not pass him in the night. They feared so they would not pass the college at night because he was there. It is said that he used to go to visit the sick, and would heal them by some mysterious power of his own. It was whispered, too, that by contrast some magic words of his could blight as well as cure, and that to incur his enmity was to destroy all hopes of happiness and life.

...To the students who came each year to study there Ole Chris became at once the most familiar figure. As his continued daily contact with the dissected and pre-dissected forms grew, his knowledge of the human anatomy took on large proportions, until eleven years ago, it is said, he was the most expert anatomist in the country. This, too, with no education whatever.

Long years ago, dark rumor has it that Chris was used to visiting the cemeteries at night when the city was asleep. New-made graves would be upturned and the form of the silent sleeper there would be removed to the Medical College to become the object of study and research. From these murmurings and reports, Ole Chris became an outcast among his race, as well as the most dreaded figure among them. The oldest physician in the city knows him well, and can recite stories of his prowess that would fill pages in a book. If all the stories about Ole Chris were to be told, his biography would fill more books than Lincoln's life or the history of the nation.

Handled Hundreds of Corpses

It will be hard to fill his place. Hundreds, and perhaps thousands, of dead bodies have been turned over to his care, and with the dexterity born of long use, he has laid them away in the brine to prepare them for dissection....

The life of Chris has many of the characteristics of a real, living ghost story. And for this reason he was feared. Negroes, some of them, believed he was a conjurer, others that he bore a mystic, charmed life. Whatever his thought may have been, whatever the motives of his peculiar life, may have had stored up in his brain, whatever objects he may have had in life, it is not known. What his power over his race, what his visions in the still hours of the night, what language he used in his conversations with the dead, only Chris himself will ever know. Certain it is that with his passing one of the most remarkable characters in the history of this country has passed silently, solemnly to dust with his secrets hidden in the mound that covers him.

A Closing Note

Though this novel ends with the death of Chris Baker, his legacy endures. Human remains of Black men, women and children found in a well near the Egyptian building in 1994 have been analyzed and interred with ceremony, but undoubtedly, other remains lie in nearby wells, including one said to be in the basement of that building. VCU has posted memorial panels at the medical school. What else might be done to honor these dead?

This story's footprint, of course, is larger than that. When driving along the tangle of highways near VCU Medical Center in downtown Richmond, your car passes over acres of defiled graves, a street once lined with markets where people were sold as livestock, and a Black neighborhood known as the Wall Street of the South split in half and ruined by those highways. Thanks to the efforts of history- and justice-minded Richmonders, however, you can park your car and walk the slave trail, pause at a lawn marking the Shockoe Bottom African Burying Ground and read a commemorative sign atop Shockoe Hill that notes the location of its successor cemetery, all within the radius of

Chris Baker's world. A few blocks of old townhomes survive from the once-bustling Jackson Ward (I recommend a visit to Maggie Walker's home, now managed by the National Parks Service). The Egyptian Building, also a protected landmark, is still in use by the medical school. Keep in mind that Chris Baker was just one of the many "anatomical men" hard at work supplying cadavers for study in the United States (and around the world). In many cases, until the mid-20th Century, no law required decent re-burial of anatomical remains.

This is not only a historical concern. To this day, a worldwide black market in body parts thrives. There is no guarantee that your corpse, or that of your loved one, will end up where you intended. The depredations of the night doctors live on.

Acknowledgments

The germ of this book came from an onboarding session for Virginia Commonwealth University's Health Hub, where I first heard of Chris Baker's career at the Medical College of Virginia. VCU university archivist and chief curator **Jodi Koste**, who has written about Baker herself, shared archival materials and links to the remarkable trove of old newspapers available online through the Library of Congress. VCU's senior curator for the Health Sciences **Margaret Kidd** kindly sent me the photographs used in this book. VCU Psychology Professor and African American Studies chairman **Shawn Utsey**, whose award-winning documentary film *Until the Well Runs Dry: Medicine and the Exploitation of Black Bodies* quite chillingly discusses 19th Century resurrectionists, with a special focus on Chris Baker (I recommend you watch the film, available on *YouTube*), encouraged me in this project and noted that, if Baker lived today, he might very well be a neurosurgeon. VCU history professor **Ryan K. Smith's** recent book *Death and Rebirth in a Southern City: Richmond's Historic Cemeteries* served as my map in tracking Chris Baker's rounds.

Thank you to the staff of the Maggie L. Walker House National Historic Site in Jackson Ward for an insightful tour, and to staff at the Library of Virginia, who provided assistance in archival newspaper research. My friends authors **Katy Munger** and **Paul Witcover**, who read an early draft and provided on point critiques that improved the book, deserve more than the occasional beer that they get in return. The sabbaticals allowed by wintry weeks at **Jeanne Wallace's** beach home in Kill Devil Hills have meant so much. I wish I could thank the anonymous person who donated her body to my anatomy dissection class at New York University. What I learned there awakened in me a new appreciation of our animate selves. Finally, I'd like to thank my wife **Christine**, who could tell by my mood at the end of each day whether I'd once again been imagining life in a basement abattoir; her understanding and care have awakened in me a new appreciation of our human hearts.

About the Author

Tony Gentry is a writer and professor emeritus in occupational therapy at Virginia Commonwealth University. Born at the Medical College of Virginia, he dissected a cadaver as an occupational therapy student, has lectured and attended meetings at the old Egyptian Building, and like most Richmonders recognizes that our history surrounds and lives in us.

Tony lives in Bon Air, down the street from Dr. Hunter McGuire's summer home, with his wife Christine and their dog Buddy.

Blog: tonygentry.com. Email: tonygentry@me.com.

References

A ghoul's confession. (1882, Dec. 15). *Richmond Dispatch.*

A study in real life. (1893, Oct. 29). *Richmond Dispatch,* 1.

Adventures with body snatchers. (1900, Apr. 8). *Richmond Times.*

Arrest of resurrectionists. *(1883, Oct. 30). National Republican, 4.*

Arrested. (1882, Dec. 15). *Staunton Vindicator,* 37:50, 4.

Asante, M.K., & Madam, A. (Eds.) (2009). *Encyclopedia of African Religions.* Sage: Thousand Oaks, CA.

Bailey, J.B. (1896). *The Diary of a Resurrectionist, 1811-1812.* Sonnenschein: London.

Baker critically ill. (1917, May 9). *Evening Journal,* 12:289, 1.

Ball, J.M. (2023). *The Sack- 'em Up Men: An Account of the Rise and Fall of the Modern Resurrectionists.* Hassell Street.

Barksdale, G., et al. (1954, Mar. 31). The legend of Chris Baker. *Scarab,* 3, 1: 3-5.

Blakely, R.L., & Harrington, J.M., eds. (1997). *Bones in the Basement: Postmortem Racism in 19th Century Medical Training.* Smithsonian: Washington, DC.

Blanton, W.B. (1933). *Medicine in Virginia in the Nineteenth Century.* Garrett & Massie: Richmond, VA.

Body-snatchers captured while in the act of robbing graves at Oakwood. (1882, Dec. 13). *State.*

Branch, M.M. (1997). *Pennies to Dollars: The Story of Maggie Lena Walker.* Linnet Books: New Haven, CT.

Campbell, B. (2012). *Richmond's Unhealed History.* Brandylane: Richmond, VA.

Chris Baker is dead: Funeral tomorrow. (1919, June 9). *Richmond News Leader,* 1.

Chris no longer feared. (1919, June 10). *News Leader,* 1.

Code of Virginia 1849 (Richmond: William F. Ritchie, 1849): Chapter 196, Section 13, p. 740; Blanton, Medicine, 69.

Cole, H. (1964). *Things for the Surgeon: A History of the Body Snatchers.* Heineman: New York.

Curl, J.S. (2000). *The Victorian Celebration of Death.* Sutton: Phoenix Mill.

Dabney, V. (1987). *Virginia Commonwealth University: A Sesquicentennial History.* University Press of Virginia: Charlottesville.

Death hovering over mysterious Chris. (1917, May 7). *The Richmond Virginian,* 1.

"DR" Chris Baker goes under surgeon's knife. (1906, Sept. 3). *News Leader,* 4622, 1.

Ezekiel, H. (1920). *The Recollections of a Virginia Newspaper Man.* Herbert T. Ezekiel: Richmond, VA.

Farrell, J. (1980). *Inventing the American Way of Death 1830-1920*. Temple University Press: Philadelphia.

Guinn, M. (2013). *The Resurrectionist*. Norton: New York.

Grand indictments. (1882, Dec. 17). *Richmond Daily Dispatch*.

Halperin, E.C. (2007). The poor, the Black, and the marginalized as the source of cadavers in United States Anatomical Education. *Clinical Anatomy*, 20: 489-495.

Hicks, S., Land, D., & McKinless, T. (2015). *Postmortem: The Story of the Richmond Grave Robber*. https://www.youtube.com/watch?v=ckaZ36zjn3Y&t=12s

Holmberg, M. (Reporter). (2010). *Meet Chris Baker, Richmond's Grave Robber* (news story). WTVR-TV: Richmond, VA https://www.wtvr.com/2010/11/17/mark-holmberg-meet-chris-baker-richmonds-grave-robber/

Jacobs, H. (2001). *Incidents in the Life of a Slave Girl*. Dover: Boston.

Jones, C. (2020). *The Organ Thieves: The Shocking Story of the First Heart Transplant in the Segregated South*. Gallery/Jeter: New York.

Kail, T. (2019). *Stories of Rootworkers & Hoodoo in the Mid-South*. History Press: Charleston, SC.

Kapsidelis, K. (2011, Nov. 11). Confronting the story of bones discovered in an old MCV well. *Richmond Times Dispatch*.

Kimball, G.D. (2003). *American City, Southern Place: A Cultural History of Antebellum Richmond*. Univ of Georgia: Athens.

Koste, J.L. (2012). *Artifacts and Commingled Skeletal Remains from a Well on the Medical College of Virginia Campus: Anatomical and Surgical Training in Nineteenth-Century Richmond*. VCU Scholars Compass.

Lee, M.D. (1966). *Virginia Ghosts*. Virginia Book Company: Richmond.

Marlowe, G.W. (2003). *A Right Worthy Grand Mission: Maggie Lena Walker and the Quest for Black Economic Empowerment*. Howard Univ. Press: Washington, DC.

Medical College of Virginia. *The First 125 Years*. Bulletin of MCV. http://scholarscompass.vcu.edu/vcu_books/2

Miller, W.I. (1997). *The Anatomy of Disgust*. Harvard U. Press: Cambridge, MA.

Mitchell, J. (1896, Jul. 11). Farewell, Solomon Marable! *Richmond Planet*, 12:30, 1.

Mitchell, J. (1896, August.1). Man and barrel. *Richmond Planet*, 12:33, 1.

Montrose, C. (2007). *Body of Work: Meditations on Mortality from the Human Anatomy Lab*. Penguin: New York.

Moore, W. (2005). *The Knife Men: Blood, Body Snatching, and the Birth of Modern Surgery*. Broadway Books: New York.

Ondaatje, M. (1984). *Coming Through Slaughter*. Penguin: New York.

Owsley, D., & Bruwelheide, K. (2012). Artifacts and Commingled Skeletal Remains from a Well on the Medical College of Virginia Campus: Introduction. *VCU Scholars Compass*.

Pember, P.Y. (1959). *A Southern Woman's Story: Life in Confederate Richmond.* McCowat-Mercer Press: Jackson, TN.

Quigley, C. (1996). *The Corpse – a History.* McFarland & Co.: Jefferson, NC.

Richardson, R. (2000). *Death, Dissection, and the Destitute.* Univ. of Chicago: Chicago.

Richmond Cemeteries. (2024). https://www.richmondcemeteries.org.

Roach, M. (2003). *Stiff: The Curious Lives of Human Cadavers.* Norton: New York.

Rozin, P., Haidt, J. & McCauley, C.R. (2008). Disgust. In M. Lewis, J.M. Haviland-Jones & L.F. Barrett (Eds.), *Handbook of Emotions*, 3rd ed. (pp. 757-776). Guilford: New York.

Sappol, M. (2002). *A Traffic of Dead Bodies: Anatomy and Embodied Social Identity in 19th Century America.* Princeton: Princeton, NJ.

Savitt, T.L. (August 1982). The use of Blacks of medical experimentation and demonstration in the Old South." *Journal of Southern History*, 48: 331-35.

Savitt, T.L. (1978). *Medicine and Slavery: The Diseases and Health Care of Blacks in Antebellum Virginia.* University of Illinois Press: Urbana.

Savitt, T.L. (2007). *Race and Medicine in Nineteenth- and Twentieth-Century America.* Kent State University Press: Kent, OH.

Schmitz, K. (2011). *A "Professor without Degrees": The Medical College of Virginia's Chris Baker.* History 490 essay, Virginia Commonwealth University. http://richmondcemeteries.org/wp-content/uploads/2012/09/Schmitz_ChrisBaker.pdf

Smith, R.K. (2020). *Death and Rebirth in a Southern City: Richmond's Historic Cemeteries.* Johns Hopkins University Press: Baltimore.

Taylor, W.H. (1871). *The Book of Travels of a Doctor of Physic.* Lippincott: Philadelphia.

The jolly medicos. (1902, Dec. 20). *Richmond Dispatch,* 10.

Trammel, J. (2012). *The Richmond Slave Trade: The Economic Backbone of the Old Dominion.* History Press: Charleston, SC.

Trammel, J., & Terrell, G. (2021). *Civil War Richmond: The Last Citadel.* History Press: Charleston, SC.

Utsey, S. & Shabazz, I. (Directors). (2011). *Until the Well Runs Dry: Medicine and the Exploitation of Black Bodies* [Film]. Burn, Baby, Burn & VCU: Richmond, VA. (YouTube: https://youtube.com/watch?v =5mV3N_fhOJs.)

Watson, J.C. and Ho, S.V. (2011). Charles Edward Brown-Sequard's departure from the Medical College of Virginia: Incompatible science or incompatible social views in pre-Civil War Southern United States. *World Neurosurgery*, 75, 5/6: 750-753.

Ward, H.M. (2012). *Public Executions in Richmond, Virginia: A History, 1782-1907.* McFarland: Jefferson, NC.

Watson, J.G. (1957, Sept.) Chris Baker: Faithful servant of medical science in Virginia. *Virginia Record,* 22-25.

References

Wilson, H.E. (1983). *Our Nig; or, Sketches from the Life of a Free Black*. Vintage: New York.

Zantac, D. (2020). *Addressing the Evidence of Historical Medical Grave Robbing: Past Practices and their Influence on Modern Memory and Western Uses of the Body.* University of Nevada: Reno, NV.

Made in the USA
Middletown, DE
11 September 2024

60718413R00158